© 

ISBN:

978-1-4477-1112-4

## Author's Notes

I've always enjoyed horror movies. I'm not sure why, really, considering the rest of my family don't really rate them that highly. If anything, they go out of their way to avoid them. I guess, if I had to give it a reason, it's because there's some faulty wiring going on somewhere deep within my little brain.

The problem is, lately, people seem to be leaning more towards horror films which rely on gore as opposed to genuine scares. Now, although I don't mind gore (unlike my brother who faints at the slightest hint of blood), I do prefer my horror to play more on my imagination with creepy imagery and things you don't see as opposed to in your face blood and guts. However, going by what some people have said on my author page (facebook search 'mattshawpublications' will take you there) it appears there is a place for gore in horror.

By writing "The Cabin" and "The Cabin II: Asylum" I gave people the horror stories which scare you by playing with your mind as opposed to overloading your senses with blood and guts. The book came out with people raving and

a number of five star reviews being awarded to it so I felt as though I had done my job well.

I didn't, though, give anything to the people who enjoy 'blood and guts' with their horror and that's where 'Consumed' comes in. This is my nod to the classic horrors I grew up with: "The Texas Chainsaw Massacre", "Braindead", "The Last House on the Left" and "I Spit On Your Grave" to name but a few.

I won't lie, I had great fun writing this piece but I do still prefer my horror with genuine frights as opposed to shocks and moments of disgust. I only hope it goes some way to satisfy the more bloodthirsty of my readers.

Enjoy! BUT...I warn you now. The sole purpose of this book was to shock and disgust the most extreme of gore-hunters whilst all the time giving them my usual entertaining storytelling style.

You've been warned.

Matt Shaw

# TOMORROW

Her dark hair, stuck to her pretty but pale face, was matted with dried blood from where they had hit her earlier; not hard enough to kill her but hard enough to ensure she stopped running and screaming from them.

Her eyes opened as she slowly regained consciousness and fear set in almost immediately as she realised she was bound, naked, to a dining room table. The blow hadn't robbed her of the memories of landing on the table - her bruised and battered body aching all over. She managed to fight her first reaction - to scream out in pain and alarm - she knew screaming wouldn't do any good; it would only let them know she was awake.

She needed time to figure out an escape.

She fought the pain in the side of her head, throbbing from the earlier blow, and started to struggle against the restraints. A dazed look down to her ankles revealed them to be bound by leather straps - perhaps fashioned from old belts? A buckle system around her ankle, she couldn't see how it was keeping her on the table - perhaps a buckle system around the table leg too? A few more seconds of

struggling against the straps and it dawned on her they weren't about to snap anytime soon.

"Shit," she muttered under her breath.

She looked up at her wrists.

A similar set-up.

"Shit!" she repeated.

Footsteps beyond the old, wooden door in the far corner of the room. They're coming. Her heart skipped a beat and she screamed when the door was pushed open.

Out of time.

# CONSUMED

## MATT SHAW

TODAY

## CHAPTER ONE

Michael walked straight past screen nine as the doors opened and the audience slowly began to filter out. He walked straight past his colleague Emma - a short, bossy woman who looked as though she should still be at school and not working in the local multiplex - and threw his broom against the door of the usher's cupboard.

"You'll need that!" Emma called over to him.

"I've finished," he called back. He didn't even look at her when he spoke, he simply continued to walk towards the staff-room where he could fetch his belongings before signing out for the night.

"You're not going to help?" Emma shouted. Michael pretended not to hear her. He could use the hustle and bustle of the leaving audience members as an excuse for his ignorance. He didn't see why he should hang around and help her. He was supposed to finish at two o'clock in the morning and it was ten to now. From past experience, he knew he'd be late leaving if he did stay and help her with

the final clean up operation. Especially considering the cinema was packed to its three hundred seat capacity. "Thanks a bunch!" Emma yelled as Michael disappeared into the male locker room. Besides - Emma never was his favourite work colleague. Despite her small size, Michael found her overbearing. What she lacked in height she made up with the volume in her voice. And where did she get off with barking orders at people as though she were part of the management team? At the end of the day she was the same level as Michael; nothing more and nothing less.

Michael couldn't help but smile as he pulled his belongings from his locker; the first smile of the day brought on by the fact it was not only the end of an extremely long ten hour shift but also because he'd never be returning to the cinema again. Not that they knew that. At the age of twenty-four, one of the oldest working there, he had always had trouble keeping hold of a job despite rarely being fired. He simply got bored with them and would walk out with little, or no, warning - often leaving his colleagues in dire straits as they'd try and manage their shift knowing they were a man down. Even if boredom hadn't taken a hold of his senses, in this particular job, he had known from the first day of working there that he wouldn't fit in. The

other staff members were in their late teens and he found it difficult to speak to them on their level. Hell, even the managers looked as though they should have still been in diapers. Some of them even acted like it too.

Two o'clock in the morning and it was still warm outside the air-conditioned building, not that Michael minded having left his home without his coat. He stood in the doorway and lit up a cigarette; a quick drag and the sickly sweet nicotine evaporated any residue stress. He dropped his silver lighter back into his trouser pocket and ran his hand through his dark brown hair. He could feel it was messed up. Another problem with the job was that they forced you to wear a baseball cap. On some people they look cool. Not on Michael. He always complained they made him look special and a few nights into working there he had already come to the conclusion they weren't even necessary; the management simply made the staff wear them to bring down their confidence a little more. With lowered confidence they'd be easier to control. No one else shared in his beliefs and he had already received two warning letters from the management for failing to turn up in the correct work uniform on the days he decided he didn't want to wear the hat. A pointless show of

disobedience, on his part, for there was always a spare hat close by for him to wear.

From across the car park a stationary van flashed its headlights catching Michael's attention in the process. Another flash of the headlights when Michael smiled and raised his hand in the air to show he had noticed it and was on his way.

"See you tomorrow," said Wayne - one of the cinema's many managers - as he stepped out of the building behind Michael.

Michael flashed him a smile as he walked down the stairs towards the car park, "I don't think so," he muttered.

"What was that?" Wayne called out after him.

"I said okay," Michael lied. He couldn't be bothered to end the evening on an argument.

He pulled the van's passenger door open as soon as he was close enough and peered in to one of his best friends, Joel.

"Put that shit out," said Joel - his green eyes fixed on the cigarette hanging from Michael's mouth.

"Can't we just open the window?" asked Michael as he jumped up onto the seat of the VW camper van.

"I mean it, put that shit out," Joel repeated. "You fucking stink."

"Jesus, deny a man his simple pleasures, Joel..." moaned Michael. He took an extra long drag before flicking the butt out of the van. "Happy?"

"You going to spend the whole weekend smoking?"

"Depends if you're going to spend the whole weekend being a miserable fuck."

There was the slightest of pauses before they both started laughing.

"How have you been?" asked Joel as he started to drive the purple vehicle out of the car park.

"Well...I'm better now I'm not going back to that shit-hole. You got my bag?"

Joel nodded, "What did they say when you told them?"

"Told them? I haven't told them anything."

"You're just not going back?" Joel was a little younger than Michael not that you'd think it if you looked at them side by side. Years working in cold garages, training as a mechanic, had ruined his complexion and he always looked as though he hadn't bothered to wash the various

engine greases from his black hair; always knotted and matted.

"Damn straight. I don't owe them any favours. You finished the van then?"

"Sort of."

"Sort of?"

"Sort of."

"Well it's looking good."

"Yeah, I got that bit fixed up okay."

The van did look good. A classic VW camper van with a funky sparkling purple paint job which certainly caught the attention of people passing by. The roof rack was a shiny chrome metal. Even the van's grill was chrome. The insides had been fixed too. The seats, once covered in torn smelly fabric, were now a lush leather - a lush leather Joel was extremely protective of even to the point of asking people to remove any keys from their back pockets before taking a seat for fear of causing a rip.

"So what bit wasn't fixed up okay?" asked Michael.

"Let's just say we nearly ended up having to get a taxi..."

"What?"

"It wouldn't start."

"But it's okay now?"

"I guess. I haven't actually switched the engine off to check if it starts again. I got it started. I figured why rock the boat?"

Michael laughed, "Don't you think it would have been a better idea to get the engine fixed first?"

"Aren't you a little old to be working in a cinema?" Joel countered.

"Ah ha! I don't work there anymore!"

"Touché! Anyway, I don't have the money to fix the engine at the moment."

"Where are we picking the others up from?" Michael asked as he made himself comfortable.

"They're all waiting at Lara's house."

"Lara?"

Joel nodded.

"She's still coming?" asked Michael.

"You know, she never wanted to come on this trip. She was only doing it to please me..."

"And now you've broken up?"

"Well now she's coming on it just to piss me off." Joel noticed Michael was looking at him with a look of concern

on his face. No doubt he was worried about the potential non-stop bickering from the ex-couple.

It wasn't just jobs Michael drifted between - it was also girlfriends - and he was a firm believer in the impossibilities of remaining friends once you had broken up with someone you'd ejaculated in. 'Lines had been crossed,' he always told people who argued that it was possible to remain friends.

"It will be fine," said Joel with what was supposed to be a reassuring smile, "we're both adults..."

\*

"Asshole." Lara was standing at the van's side door. It was the first time she had seen Joel since he had unceremoniously dumped her via text message; an act brought about by lack of phone credit as opposed to cowardice - not that Lara believed him and certainly not what she told their mutual friends who preferred to simply not get involved.

"Whore." Joel's insult was merely a reaction to being called an asshole. He didn't believe Lara was a whore. He had been her first love and knew she hadn't seen anyone

since they had broken up. As soon as the word escaped his lips he regretted it - not that he wanted her to know.

"Okay, you can sit right at the back," said Hayley - another of the group - as she pushed Lara into the seats towards the back of the van; the furthest point from Joel.

Hayley and Lara were complete opposites; whilst Hayley was a natural blonde, with brain cells to match, Lara was dark haired and highly intelligent. Hayley was stunningly attractive whereas you had to look deep to see any beauty in Lara - that's not saying it wasn't there, it was just well hidden underneath the shield she continually put up to protect herself from the assholes of the world. A shield which Joel saw straight through after initial, careful navigation. Hayley never left home without a full face of carefully applied make-up - used expertly to enhance her model-like looks - and Lara never left home with make-up. Even when she and Joel were dating she still preferred the natural look as opposed to a look which gave the impression of being too 'try-hard'.

It would be a safe assumption that neither Hayley nor Lara would have been friends had it not been for their mutual acquaintances.

With Lara tucked into the corner of the back row of seats, Hayley climbed up onto the row of seats behind the driver's seat.

"They haven't started already, have they?" asked Dan. He jumped into the seat next to his girlfriend, Hayley, and turned to Lara. "You haven't started already, have you? You'll never win him back at that rate..."

"I wouldn't take him back," she hissed.

Michael leaned over to Joel and whispered in his ear, "Dude - she hates you...What did you say to her?"

"Not a lot. I only had enough credit to send the one text."

"You text her?"

Joel nodded.

Michael couldn't help but laugh, "That's awesome."

Lara called from the back seat, "I can hear you, you know..."

Dan carried on pestering her, "Did you save the text? Can I read it?"

"Fuck off, Dan..." she hissed.

Charlotte, the final member of the group, climbed into the van and took her seat next to Lara, "Please stop arguing," she urged. The youngest girl of the group,

Charlotte hated anything to do with arguments or ill-feelings. Protected from the harsh realities of life, like arguments between friends, by her parents - the others often felt the need to try and protect her too. Anything to stop her from bursting into tears - something she was often prone to doing and often without much cause. "You said everything would be cool between you guys."

"It will be," said Lara. She turned to look out of the window, "As soon as he drops dead. Okay. I'm sorry. It's out of my system now."

"Look..." Joel went to argue.

"You're talking to me? You sure you wouldn't prefer to send me a text? I haven't changed my number yet," she retorted, cutting him short.

Michael leaned across and whispered, "Because she's still hoping you'll text an apology and go back out with her."

"Not happening," Joel whispered back. "Not got any credit, for one."

"Come on already!" shouted Dan. "Let's get this show on the fucking road already! We'll never get there! Come on! Come on! Come on!"

"Okay!" Joel shouted back. "Charlotte, did you tie the bags in properly on the roof-rack?"

Michael turned to look at Charlotte; sitting in the back playing with her dark hair - twiddling her ponytail between her fingers - something she often did when she was nervous. He turned back to Joel. "You seen the way her pony-tail is tied back?"

"What's wrong with my hair?" asked Charlotte.

Michael turned back to her, "Nothing, it looks lovely. I'm just saying he may want to give the knots a quick check before we set off. Be a shame to get to the site only to find everything has fallen off back where we set off."

"They'll be fine," said Charlotte as she continued playing with her ponytail. Joel gave her a quick glance in the rear-view mirror. Seconds later he jumped from the driver's seat to give the ropes a quick check. "Jesus Christ, I do know how to fasten things to roof racks properly!"

Michael laughed and gave Charlotte a big, cheesy grin.

"I've got a question," asked Dan - sitting in between them. "Are you two finally going to fuck and get it out of your system on this break, or what?"

"Me and her?" said Michael. "She wishes..."

"Uh huh...okay then, lover-boy," said Dan with a grin on his face. He knew the constant bullying, from Michael to Charlotte, was nothing more than a playground mentality. He knew because it was exactly what he used to do with Hayley. In the end though Hayley was too slow to notice any kind of signal from Dan so he had resorted to plying her with wine until she was bordering on unconsciousness for their first kiss...and more.

"Oh my God!" said Charlotte. She tried to hide her reddening face behind her hair. Unlike Hayley she wasn't too slow to notice any signals. She just wasn't used to receiving them in such a way and so, most of the time, they went over her head. A late starter in the romance department thanks to attending an all girls' school until the age of eighteen.

"All good!" said Joel as he jumped into the driver's seat. "Ready or not...Here we go!"

A cheer from Dan and Hayley. Lara was still sulking about having to share a van with Joel. Michael was staying silent hoping his denial of fancying Charlotte was enough to kill the conversation for the rest of the trip. Charlotte was wondering what she had let herself in for by agreeing to come on this trip in the first place.

The plan was simple. Drive through the early hours of the morning when traffic would be minimal and get to the campsite in time for a morning fry-up. The van reached the end of the road, the indicator flashing to all those nearby that they were about to turn left to head off towards the countryside.

Dan piped up from his seat, "Dude, I need to take a piss."

# CHAPTER TWO

'In 200 yards, turn left' chirped the female voice on the satellite navigation system, which had been suckered onto the middle of the van's windscreen.

"Do we have to listen to that the whole way?" whined Michael - already irritated by the female's robotic voice, despite only being on the road for five minutes.

"Well that is the whole point of sat navs; turn them on, when you're ready to leave, put in the destination and - hey presto - follow the instructions until you arrive safely," said Joel without even taking his eyes off the road.

There was a pause before Michael suddenly burst out with, "Yeah - fuck that." Before Joel had a chance to realise what Michael was doing, he pulled the sat nav system off the window, switched it off, and threw it in the back of the van, "Head's up back there!"

"Whoa! What are you doing! I need that!" moaned Joel.

"No, you don't. You've got something better than a crappy little satellite navigation...You've got me. I know the way." said Michael - an air of arrogance in his voice.

"Yeah, thanks but I'd rather have..."

Michael cut him off mid-sentence, "You realise those little machines...They take you miles out of your way."

"Sorry but I have to call bullshit on that one," Dan chipped in from the seat behind Michael's. "You can program them in so they take you the most direct route."

"Big companies...You know...The real big boys...Like McDonalds...KFC...even the main supermarket chains...They're in with the people who make those little boxes."

"What?!" Joel said.

"They pay them a substantial amount of money, I'm not sure whether it's yearly or monthly or...whatever...They pay them a fuck load of money to ensure we, the drivers using the maps, are forced to drive past the various companies...All it takes is ten percent of us drivers to stop off and make a purchase...That's a lot of money thanks to a forced route."

"Really?" asked Hayley.

"No. Not really," said Dan, "that's complete shit."

Joel called out to the back, "Can someone please just pass it back through?" he turned to Michael, "Can you put it back on the windscreen, please?"

"No!" barked Michael. He addressed the back of the van, "I swear, you pass that through, I'll throw it out of the window." He turned back to Joel who was still driving, "You just missed your turning."

Joel was visibly getting stressed, "This is ridiculous."

"Come on, trust me, I know a short cut. Turn right just up here, you can get back on route."

"Fine but you're paying the extra fuel money if we get lost."

"We won't get lost. Trust me."

*

Joel was sitting in the driver's seat still. The early morning sun illuminating his face - showing his irritation clearly to all those who glanced at him. Once comfortable, now he wanted nothing more than to swap with someone else so he could relax and de-stress from the journey already traveled - not that he'd swap with anyone else...Not whilst they were in his VW camper van. No one got to drive other than him. He was looking out of the window, staring towards a petrol station they had stumbled across - the only building they had seen for what felt like hours. A building

that they were all surprised to see was open for business when they pulled up outside. On first impressions it looked as though it was derelict - ready for demolition. The back half of the building, visible as you drove up to the property, already looked as though it had been partly demolished.

"Just relax," said Hayley, "it's all part of the fun. And, on the bright side, we're getting to see lots of new places."

"I don't want to see lots of new places," hissed a clearly stressed Joel, "I want to see the campsite. I want to see the campsite. I want to see a nice pint of cider. I even want to see a warm sleeping bag...A comfortable pillow..."

"And I wanted a real man...I guess we can't have everything we want, hey?" snapped Lara. Unlike Joel, she wasn't stressed from the journey. She was already stressed simply from being in the same vehicle as Joel.

"Fuck off," said Joel.

A bell, above the petrol station's door, chimed - alerting everyone in the van that the door had been opened. Joel turned his attention back to the station's entrance and watched as Michael stepped out, back into the fading daylight; a sheepish look on his face.

He crossed the forecourt and jumped into the front of the van, back onto the passenger seat, next to where Joel was sitting - and fuming.

"Well?" barked Joel.

"The funniest thing..." said Michael. He tried his best not to laugh, sensing Joel's annoyance.

"How far?"

"Did you want that in miles or kilometers?"

"Cut the shit, Mike, how far out of the way have you taken us?"

The satellite navigation system had informed Joel the journey should have taken approximately four hours. So far, they had been on the road for just under six - extra time which was eating, slowly, into their camping trip.

"Relax," said Michael, "if you think about it...We're only camping...It's not as though we're staying in a hotel. We could pitch up anywhere and have a nice weekend...We don't have to go to that particular site...We could find another...One that's closer..."

"We agreed on this site," said Joel. "We paid for space at this site...Now...Tell me, before I have to kill you...Where the fuck are we?"

"We're about an hour in the wrong direction... About...Give or take...An hour...Or two..."

Joel turned to Dan, in the seats behind them, "Pass me the sat nav, will you?"

Dan knew when to keep his mouth shut and simply passed the little box over to Joel. With no further words, he snatched it and secured it to the windscreen again. He stopped when he saw Michael start to put his seat-belt back on, "What are you doing?"

"Safety. You know, if we get pulled over and I'm not wearing a seat-belt...I can get a fine..."

"Fuel."

"I'm sorry?"

"We agreed, you pay the extra fuel costs if we get lost. Well, we're lost...We're running low on fuel...And, oh look, we're at a petrol station...The chances!"

"They're out."

"What?"

"Yeah, they don't have any fuel..." Michael finished putting his seat-belt on.

"Did you think to ask where the nearest petrol station was?"

"No, but there is a McDonalds about ten miles that way," Michael helpfully pointed up the road. "Happy Meals all round?"

Dan helpfully pointed out, "We're supposed to be at the site already. We should have been tucking into a nice healthy heart-attack fry-up..."

Michael, "McDonalds could still be serving breakfast. What time is it?"

Joel shook his head, "You're a dick. Really. You are." He turned to the back of the van, "Lara, did you want to sit up here with me? Perhaps you could carry on calling me an asshole for the rest of the road trip? Yeah? Let's really make it a trip to remember."

Lara replied by raising her middle finger.

Michael leaned closer to Joel, "Come on, man, we'll be laughing about this around the campfire in a few hours."

Joel turned the satellite navigation system on and sat back, waiting for it to book up properly, "You're a dick, Mike...A dick. We'd have already been there. Tents would have been set up. Fry-up consumed. Laughter. Fun. Maybe we would have even had a little walk..." He addressed the rest of the group, "Everyone ready?"

The group, with the exception of Michael, agreed unenthusiastically. Clearly they were all wishing they hadn't chosen to go with Michael's own internal map system.

With no warning a hand slammed against the glass window on the driver's side. They all jumped as no one had seen the person approach. Joel turned to see a rough looking man peering in. His clothes were tatty, his face was gaunt and unshaven, his dark brown hair messed up as though he had recently crawled through a hedge backwards.

Joel wound the window down, "Can I help you?"

"Sorry, I didn't mean to startle you...Was just wondering if you guys could help me out..."

"What's up?" Dan called from the middle section of the van.

The stranger leaned in, making Joel feel uncomfortable in the process, to address Dan, "Hi...Sorry...It's just that I..." The stranger stopped when he saw Hayley. He couldn't help but smile at her beauty. She, in turn, smiled back at him - more out of politeness than anything else. "Oh, hi..." the man said.

"Hi," said Hayley.

"You were saying?" asked Joel. He shifted forward in his seat forcing the stranger to pull his head out of the van.

"I broke down a little down the way. Just walked down here to use the phone...Just wondered if you'd mind driving me back to my car. My brother's picking me up with his tow truck..."

"You didn't think to ask him to collect you from here?"

The stranger paused. "No. No, I didn't. So...A lift?"

Hayley leaned forward, "He seems nice enough...Give him a...."

Joel cut her off, "I'm sorry. We don't even know you..."

"Does that matter?" the stranger asked. "It's just a few miles in that direction..."

Joel continued, "And we're running late. Not a lot of fuel...Heading in that direction. I'm sorry."

"Come on, it'll take you ten minutes max..."

"And I'm sure it won't take you long to walk it. I'm sorry."

Joel pressed his foot on the accelerator before the man could say anything and the van pulled away from the petrol station's tatty forecourt.

"Whoa! What's all that about!" Dan said from behind Joel and Michael.

"We don't have the time or the petrol," Joel spat - his temper frayed.

"That's cold," Dan moaned.

"And if we run empty," Joel said to Michael, "you're pushing. Got it?"

# CHAPTER THREE

Joel was sat, twisted in his seat, staring at Michael who was refusing to budge.

"You weren't joking?" asked Michael.

Joel didn't say anything. He let the stern, pissed off, expression on his face do the talking.

Lara called out from the back of the van, "I don't have any signal either." A quick look on their phones revealed none of them had any network coverage with which to call for help.

"I'm not pushing," said Michael. He looked out of the windscreen at the road ahead which seemed to stretch for miles and miles - as far as the eye could so. Nothing but fields and trees in the distance - the latter hiding signs of any civilization. "I'm sure someone will be along any minute."

"Well let's hope they deal with stranded people better than we did," said Dan.

"If we had helped him, we'd have broken down sooner!" Joel replied indignantly.

"Which, in turn, meant we'd have been closer to the petrol station..." Dan continued.

"Would that be the same petrol station which had run out of fuel?" asked Joel.

"At least they had a telephone," Dan fired back.

"I thought all the arguments had stopped now?" whined Charlotte.

"That's before I realised what a cock Michael was," said Joel.

"What the fuck?! I wasn't even arguing - it was Dan!" Michael pointed out.

Joel opened the van door and stepped onto the road. Without saying anything else, he turned and slammed the door shut.

"So what now?" asked Hayley.

"Now he gets to breathe some fresh country-air in and calm down," said Lara. "He'll be fine in a minute." Lara knew better than anyone else in the van how hot-headed Joel could get when he was stressed. She also knew it never took a lot to get him to that level either. "Just give him some space."

Michael didn't say anything, he just sat there with a sheepish look upon his face.

"And then what?" Hayley continued.

"And then we continue sitting here, waiting for someone to come by...Or...Or we pitch the tents up in one of those fields..."

"Because that will help get the van fixed?" asked Charlotte.

"It will give us somewhere to stay for the night. Michael can sit up and keep watch for passing traffic," Dan pointed out.

"Seems fair," said Lara.

Michael turned to her, "And you wonder why Joel sent you that text?"

"Fuck you."

"And what if we don't want to go with any of those options?" asked Charlotte - ignoring the potential argument between Lara and Michael.

"Well then I guess we have a hike...Pick a direction and head off to try and find some help...Or a phone to get help. I don't know...I didn't put us in this position and I don't have the answers...Jesus..." Dan opened the door and stepped out to join Joel. He too slammed the door. Not because he was in a mood with anyone, he just couldn't be

dealing with anymore of their questions. Especially when he didn't have the answers they desperately wanted.

"What's wrong with him?" asked Charlotte.

"Might be my fault," said Hayley. "Before we left he wanted...Well...You know...But we couldn't. He always gets grumpy when I say no - as though I plan when to start my period just so I can deny him what he believes to be his right to sex."

"You couldn't just give him a quick hand-job?" asked Michael. "Use your mouth?"

Charlotte made a disapproving noise, from the back of her throat, as though the mere talk of hand-jobs and blow-jobs offended her. A disapproving noise which was, mostly, ignored by the rest of her friends.

"And get myself turned on in the process? Like that's fair! He can wait. It's not as though it's normally for more than three or four days."

"And there's always the arse..." Michael chirped, wondering how far he could push Hayley. "Unless you're one of these women who saves that for special occasions like Christmas and birthdays…"

"Joel was right," said Hayley, "you're a dick." She opened her door and jumped out. The other girls didn't wait around for Michael to start on them and also left the van.

"And now I'm sitting here all alone," said Michael. He waited for a couple more seconds, "Yep...All alone...Fuck this." He joined the rest of the group in the middle of the road.

Joel was in the middle of apologising, "I'm sorry...It's been a long night and I'm just tired."

Michael caught the tail end of the conversation as he closed the van door behind him and offered, "Want me to drive?"

Joel sighed, "Please can someone just shut him up? Please?"

Michael continued, "Come on, I'm sorry. I'm sorry. There, I said it. I'm sorry. I didn't mean for us to get lost. I didn't mean for us to run out of petrol. It's happened, we just need to stick together and deal with it. Like I said, we'll be laughing about it in hours to come. We just need to stick together and plan what to do. There's no point arguing about it."

"He's right," said Charlotte - she hoped his apology and Joel's previous apology would be the first steps to

getting the rest of the group to calm down and get their holiday back on track. "This was supposed to be a fun weekend, let's not ruin it."

"So where do we go from here?" asked Joel.

"Are you sure the van ran out of fuel?" Michael asked.

"Yes, I'm sure," replied Joel with a patronising tone in his voice.

"You say that but earlier you told me you had troubles starting the van...All that money to make it look good and yet nothing spent making it run as well as it could. Maybe something snapped under the hood?"

"You were having troubles with the van and you didn't think to say anything?" Lara seized the opportunity to get involved.

"Yes, yes I was having troubles with the van. But I got it running again. And then we ran out of fuel. The orange light came on warning it was low ages ago...I'm telling you, we are running on empty."

"As I said to the girls in the van, we have a choice. We can pitch up here and wait for someone to pass us by. It's still early. This road could get busier later on. Or...Or we could pick a direction and head off to try and find a phone

or someone who could help us. Finally we could just stand around here playing the blame game. Personally, I reckon we should pick a direction and start walking - for all we know there could be a petrol station just a little way over there behind the trees."

"Or we could sit here and wait for someone to pass," said Joel, "and Michael can go and see if he can find someone to help."

"Whatever we decide," Michael said, "we should stick together. What if I went off into the woods and I was attacked by a bear?"

"A bear? Seen many bears in England?" asked Lara.

Michael shrugged, "Doesn't mean they aren't out there. Could be really good at disguise."

Charlotte blurted out, "Let's take a vote." Anything to stop another round of trying to get one up over each other in the argument stakes. "I say we go for a little walk and see what we can find. What about you?" she turned to Lara.

"We should wait. At least for a bit. As Dan said, it's early at the moment. Could get busier here later on."

"I'll walk with you," said Michael. In fairness, he didn't need to answer. As soon as Charlotte had cast her

vote - it was clear to the group which way Michael would go.

"Surprise," muttered Dan. "Look...Why don't you two walk to the tree line and see if you can see anything in the distance. If you can't then come back and Hayley and I will walk through one of the other fields and see if we can spot anything, in the distance, which may be of use...But we won't head off until you're back. Otherwise we could all get lost or all end up calling people out. That way we get all directions covered and leave people at the van just on the off chance anyone drives on by. Sound like a plan?" They all nodded - much to Dan's relief. "And don't forget to keep checking your phone whilst you're walking," he told Charlotte and Michael, "just because there's no signal here - it doesn't mean there won't be any a little further down there. Might save yourselves a walk."

"Sounds good to me," said Michael - as though he was going to argue against having to spend time alone with Charlotte.

"Just try not to rape her when you get to the woods," Dan pointed out, a wry smile on his face.

"What?" an alarmed look on Charlotte's face.

"Fuck you!" Michael spat.

"I was joking," Dan reassured Charlotte. "We all know Mike would never have been able to pin you!"

"Fuck you!" Michael spat once again.

The group laughed at Michael's expense.

"Yeah, well, if I do happen to try it on and I do succeed...You only have yourselves to blame...Egging me on like that," said Michael. He turned to Charlotte, "Let's go." He didn't wait for an answer. He simply started walking in the direction of the nearest line of trees, at the far side of the field on the left hand side of the road.

"I don't suppose anyone has a whistle I can blow on if he tries anything?" asked Charlotte - part of her joking, part of her deadly serious. The group took it as a joke and laughed it off as Charlotte started to walk after Michael.

"We'll sound the horn if anyone comes down the road," Joel called out after them.

Michael raised his hand in acknowledgement.

"So now what?" Joel asked as he turned back to the rest of the group. Immediately he noticed that Hayley and Dan had climbed back into the van, and closed the doors behind them and it was just Lara standing with him. "Oh..." he said.

"It's okay. You don't have to talk to me," said Lara. "You have the perfect excuse not to, after all...No mobile phone signal. You couldn't possibly send me a text message."

"You're never going to let me forget that, are you?" said Joel. It was more of a rhetorical question but she answered anyway.

"You think I'm ever going to forget that my first proper boyfriend dumped me via text message? Worse still - completely out of the blue."

"I did say sorry," he pointed out.

"No. No I don't think you did," said Lara - clearly annoyed.

"Well for what it's worth, I am sorry."

There was a pause as Lara waited for him to follow his apology up with a joke of some description. No joke came. "Thank you," she said.

"And I promise not to dump my next girlfriend via text," he joked.

Lara rolled her eyes.

\*

"You don't believe what they said, do you?" Michael asked Charlotte as they walked, side by side, through the country field of tall grass, towards the tree line on the horizon.

"That you'll rape me?" she asked. She shook her head. "If I thought that...Firstly we wouldn't be friends and secondly, I wouldn't be walking towards a forest with you..."

"I actually meant about me fancying you..." he said sheepishly. It hadn't even crossed his mind that she may have taken the previous conversations about 'rape' seriously.

"What? No. No," she said.

"Because I don't," he continued.

"Oh, thanks. Good to know..."

"No...You know...You're not my type..."

"Great. Anything else? Fat arse? Ugly?"

"No...Nothing like that. I just prefer blondes," he continued - completely unaware of the hole he was digging for himself. "It's not because you're ugly. Because, you know, you're not. Just, not for me..."

"Awesome," she said in a completely monotone voice.

"I'm sure you'll find someone though. Some day." He meant it as a compliment despite how it came out.

"You think?" she asked sarcastically. "I do so hope so," she continued, "I dream about it..."

"Well it will happen. No sense rushing it..."

"Look," she said, "why don't we walk in silence? Enjoy the peace and quiet of the countryside. It's nice. Listen," she lifted her hand to her ear and paused to take in the tranquility.

"I can't hear anything," said Michael missing the point completely.

Charlotte changed the subject, "Do you have any signal on your phone yet?" she asked as she checked her own mobile phone.

Michael fished his mobile from his pocket and gave it a check - still no service. He shook his head and started to walk again with Charlotte a few steps behind him - wishing she had stayed by the van with the others.

*

Joel shook his head in disgust, at the sight of Haley and Dan making out in the van, "If they stain the seats..."

"At least someone is having a nice time on this trip," said Lara. She walked over to the roadside and sat on the grass verge.

Joel walked over and sat next to her, "Is it really that bad?"

"Look where we are," she pointed out. "Has the holiday even started?"

"At least we're talking," said Joel, "so one good thing has come from it already."

"You've calmed down from earlier."

"You know me. I blow up and calm down pretty soon afterwards."

"Same old, same old...One day you might learn to grow up a bit."

Joel smiled, he let her get away with the slur. She did, after all, know him better than anyone else on the trip. Part of him even believed she knew him better than he knew himself.

"You know I regretted that text more or less as soon as I sent it," he told her - his voice hesitant as to whether he should be admitting any of this.

"What?"

"I was angry. Can't even remember what set me off."

"You dumped me because you were in a mood?" she asked. Her facial expression pointed out how she felt about this - her tone of voice backed it up.

"I remember being gutted a few hours later. I wanted to call you and explain...I had made a mistake...I..."

"You had made a mistake?" Lara pounced on his words.

Joel nodded. "That's how I felt. Wished I could take the text back."

"You didn't think to call me? Talk to me?"

"Would you have answered even if I had?"

"Probably," she pointed out, "even if it were just to shout at you."

"Fair point."

"And you don't remember why you sent me the text?"

"That's the really tragic thing about it," he laughed - more of a laugh of embarrassment. "So...Have you been seeing anyone?" he asked. Joel already knew the answer. Their mutual friends often let slip how miserable Lara had been since they stopped going out - which made Joel distance himself from them. He didn't need the extra feelings of guilt tied in with his feelings of stupidity for sending the text in the first place. He had been doing okay,

since leaving Lara, as he rarely saw her; it was easier to put her out of mind, although it still hurt. Since picking her up, though, with the others - slowly he had begun to remember the reasons why he had originally dated her, despite the fact she had been giving him a hard time. He could forgive her for treating him badly that morning. He knew, as soon as he pressed 'send' on the text message, it would upset her.

"Have you been seeing anyone?" she asked.

He shook his head. She didn't need to know about the series of one-night stands he had 'enjoyed' since splitting with her. Lara didn't know the girls he had slept with so there was no danger of her ever finding out and it would only cause her more upset.

"You should have just called me," she said. "We could have talked..."

"Just didn't seem fair."

"I loved you," she pointed out. "Some nights I hated you and some nights I wished you would have called. I loved you," she repeated.

"Well...I love you," he said throwing all caution to the wind.

"What?"

"Seeing you today just makes me realise what a mistake I made...The old feelings I had for you - they're still there..."

"I don't believe it..."

"I know, right..Who would have thought it?"

"No, look!" she pointed further down the road towards an oncoming truck.

# CHAPTER FOUR

"Okay, I do like you," Michael said as he suddenly span around to face Charlotte. Charlotte stopped dead.

"That's good to know, I like you too," she said. She always knew Michael had the potential to be a little quirky but today she was seeing him in a whole new light.

"No...I mean obviously I like you but I meant to say...I like you. You know, more than a friend."

Charlotte smiled as she felt her face redden. She wasn't so much blushing at the sudden announcement of feelings towards her, more so because of the way they were being made clear to her. Michael, the quirky bull in a china shop. Next up she wondered whether he was just going to follow-up his 'love' for her by reaching in and trying to fondle a breast.

"Well?" he asked. It was clear from his facial expression that he was hoping she was going to return the sentiment but she just stood there with the very same nervous smile on her face.

In Charlotte's mind she had often wondered how this conversation would have gone. She pictured Michael to be

capable of being extremely charming and romantic - especially considering he was often thought of as being some kind of modern-day Casanova amongst their friends who often told tales of his amazing ability at pulling the members of the opposite sex on crazy nights out. Now she could only picture him, in a club, sneaking rohypnol into the ladies' drinks and waiting for them to fall unconscious so he could get his leg over. She opened her mouth, as though about to give him his answer, when she was suddenly disturbed by the sound of a horn - coming from across the field, back on the main road.

"Someone must have shown up," she pointed out, with a barely audible sigh of relief that she hoped Michael didn't pick up on. "Quick!" she about turned and started to run back towards the road - hopeful that all mention of the previous conversation would disappear, forgotten, by the time they rejoined the rest of the group.

By the time the two of them crossed the field, the 'help' had already pulled up; a large pick-up truck with a car already being towed behind it. The driver, and his passenger, jumped out.

"Well, well, well...Isn't this a turn-up," said the passenger; the same man whom Joel had refused to help at the petrol station earlier.

"Shit," Joel muttered under his breath.

"What seems to be the trouble?" asked the other man - the driver of the truck.

Even if the stranger they had met earlier at the petrol station hadn't mentioned the fact he wanted to call for his brother, you'd have been able to tell they were brothers just by looking at them. The only difference between the two of them was that the brother with the tow truck looked older. He had more specks of grey in his dark hair - longer hair than his brother's at near shoulder length.

"We ran out of petrol," said Dan.

"Too bad, petrol station is miles away," said the younger of the brothers - the one they had abandoned earlier.

"Hush now, Johnny," said the other brother.

"Stephen...These fucks..." Johnny fell silent as his brother, Stephen, shot him a look.

"You'll have to excuse my brother," said Stephen. "He's been stuck with his car most of the night."

"Because they wouldn't help me...." Johnny moaned under his breath.

Joel spoke up, "Look we're sorry. As you can see, we clearly didn't have the petrol to help out. We didn't even make it to our destination!"

"There you go," said Johnny, "they apologised." He addressed Joel, "Although, had you helped him...You'd have been a lot closer to the nearest petrol station..."

"We don't know the area, we're only over this way because we got lost," said Joel.

"Regardless, it doesn't matter...Doesn't change a damned thing now, does it?" Johnny continued, a smile on his face. "Anyway, as you can see, I'm already helping my brother out...Unless of course you'd like for me to leave his car here whilst we tow you to a petrol station?"

Dan could tell by the expression on Joel's face that he was desperate to agree that this was a good idea; leave the car there and tow them to get some fuel. He jumped in before Joel had a chance to annoy the strangers so much that they'd just leave them there stranded, "How about you give us a ride to the nearest? We could just hitch a lift until one of us has enough phone signal to make a call...Get some

help? Or, if we happen to get to a station first, we could jump out there?"

"No petrol stations where we're going," said Johnny. "We only live a little way from here. Sorry."

Johnny turned away from the group and returned to the passenger seat of the tow truck. Once in, he slammed the door behind him.

Stephen made an excuse, "You'll have to excuse him. He always gets cranky when he's tired and hungry. He's right, though, we only live down the road. Tell you what, I could drive him home...I could dump his car...Come back for you and take you where ever you want...How's that grab you?"

"Or we could come with you...Make a call from your place, if that's okay, and then...You wouldn't have to come back out. If you only live down the road, we could walk back..." said Michael - sensing that neither brother would return for them.

"Or we could get someone to collect us from your place?" Dan offered.

Stephen turned his attention to Hayley. "Come back to our place?"

"Probably be easier that way," Michael said.

Hayley shifted uneasily under the continuing gaze of the stranger.

"I'm not sure," said Stephen. He looked back to Michael. "I'll have to check with my brother. You okay to wait a minute?"

"Sure," said Dan.

"Thanks," Stephen walked over to the tow truck and jumped in next to his brother. He closed the door behind him so none of the group - watching on - could hear what was being said.

"Of all the people to show up," said Joel.

"Just play it cool," Dan told him. "We need to make the best of this situation. Unless...Unless you'd rather be sitting here for the rest of the day?"

"No, I'd rather be at the camp-site," he said. He fired Michael a look to remind him that this was all his fault. Michael smiled.

The driver's door opened and Stephen stepped down onto the road.

"Okay - hop in," said Stephen. "You might have to sit on each others' laps but...Should be enough room for you all to squeeze in," he continued.

"What about our stuff?" asked Joel.

"Your stuff? Yeah, we aren't going to fit that in," said Stephen. "Seriously though, look around...It isn't going anywhere...We'll be back in about thirty minutes or so...I'll take you back to my house...We'll off-load my brother's car...We'll come back and tow you to the nearest petrol station. Your stuff will still be here..."

"I'll wait here," said Joel, "at least we won't all have to squeeze in together...One of us should wait."

"Up to you," said Stephen, "I'm not going to twist your arm to come. All of you can stay, if you want..."

Joel turned to the rest of the group, "I'll wait here..."

Dan stepped over to the tow-truck, "I'll come with you," he told Stephen.

"Me too," said Hayley.

Stephen smiled, "So that's settled...Unless anyone else wants to come along for the ride too?"

Charlotte stepped forward, "I'll come," she said - not because she felt it was necessary to go, she just wanted to get away from anymore awkward conversations with Michael.

"Okay, jump on in then," said Stephen. He opened the back door of the tow-truck so his new passengers could climb aboard. Dan was first in, followed by Hayley and

Charlotte. Stephen closed the door behind Charlotte and climbed into the front seat.

The engine of the tow-truck kicked into life as he wound down the window to talk to Joel, "So we'll be back in about thirty minutes. You guys just hang tight and don't go anywhere."

Joel nodded.

"Thank you," said Lara. She felt as though someone should say it and it was clear Joel wasn't going to be the first in line to offer up some thanks for reasons unknown to her.

"My pleasure," Stephen smiled. "What kind of human being would I be if I had just left you guys stranded?" He gave Lara a wink as the tow-truck pulled away from the conked out van.

"What was all that about?" Lara asked Joel.

"What?"

"You were rude. They're helping us out and you were rude."

"No, I wasn't."

"You were a little bit," Michael chipped in.

"You know what, I don't want to hear from you - this is your fault. Go for a walk, or something," Joel told Michael.

"What's wrong with you?" said Lara. "You're like Dr Jekyll and Mr Hyde...One minute all nice - sweet even..."

"When was that?" Michael asked.

"The next, you're back to being a bastard!" she finished.

"I'm tired," said Joel, "and I don't trust them. There's something about them. Had we all gone with them - they'd probably have called one of their friends to come and take anything of worth from the van...It's in the papers all the time, that sort of crime."

"Well I don't know what papers you've been reading," Lara said. She turned her back on Joel and climbed back into the van. Once in, she laid down on the row of seats at the back.

"Shit," Joel muttered. He had only just made it up with Lara, he didn't want to ruin things again. Especially if he had any chance of fixing their broken relationship.

"What's going on between you two?" Michael asked, picking up the mixed feelings between them.

"Just give us a minute," said Joel. He walked over to the van and clambered up onto the seats in front of where Lara lay. He closed the door behind him to ensure Michael didn't follow. "I'm sorry," he told Lara. She didn't reply. She just laid there, on the back seat, with her eyes closed. "Did you hear me?"

"Yes. Two apologies in one day. You must be coming down with something."

"I meant what I said earlier," he told her. He kept one eye on Michael to make sure he wasn't listening to the private conversation but he needn't have worried for Michael had turned his attention to throwing stones across the road. "I know it's too late and the feelings aren't mutual but...I do...I do still love you."

"What do you want from me?" she asked without so much as moving. "Am I supposed to leap up and profess my undying love for you? Are we supposed to pick up from where you dropped us, as though it never happened? The two of us together forever? Back to boyfriend and girlfriend, married with kids before we know it...Live a long happy life, growing old together whilst watching our children continue in our footsteps...Starting their own family? Is that it?"

"What if I said yes?" he asked.

"What? I don't have time for your games," she moaned.

"Not a game. What if I said I did want to marry you? What if I told you that all this time, without you...I've been miserable. I know you have too...The time apart just made me realise how much I loved you...Helped by seeing you today..."

She opened her eyes to look at him, "You're being serious?"

He nodded, "Marry me."

"Do you know how ridiculous you sound?"

"I don't care. We've wasted enough time."

"We?"

"I..."

"We can't get married," she told him. "We're too young for starters..."

"My folks got married early. They're still together."

"And mine are divorced so that must tell you what I think about the institution of marriage."

"We could get engaged at least," he pressed - desperation oozing from his voice.

"Do you have any idea how you are sounding at the moment?"

"I'm sounding like someone who is in love. Look, I want you. I know that now. I'm sorry for leaving you. I truly am. If I could take it back I would. Honestly. But I can't. I just need for you to forgive me and say you'll give it another go...That you want to give it another go..."

"And what if I don't want to?" she asked.

He paused.

"What if I said okay to us getting back together and then you went and dumped me again? Do you know how much that hurt? How many nights I cried myself to sleep? Any idea?"

"It won't happen again, I promise. I swear. You're the one I want. We were great together, you know we were. And we're meant to be together. If not then you'd have met someone else. Or I would have...But neither of us did, in the time we weren't together. Come on, a speed bump, that's what it was. We just need to get over it. I won't let you down again. I won't hurt you again."

Lara sat up and rested her back against the back of the seat.

"I need to think," she said. "This is all happening too fast." And it was happening too fast. She had woken, that morning, hating him for what he had done for her. Deep down she knew she still loved him but what if he did dump her unceremoniously, by text, again? She knew she couldn't take it a second time. Part of her wanted to tell him they could have another go but the other part of her feared they'd just be kidding themselves and the chances of them having a relationship were doomed from the offset.

Joel desperately wanted to push her for an answer but knew, to do so, would be to push her away. "Okay," he said, "well...Take as long as you need," he said. He only hoped that she didn't need too long to think about it as he wanted nothing more than to cradle her in his arms once more. And some petrol for his van.

# CHAPTER FIVE

The tow-truck turned off the road and slowly made its way up a dirt-track towards a large, nice looking house which was set back against some woodlands.

"You guys live here?" Dan asked from the back seat.

"Whole family does," said Stephen. Johnny simply muttered - still annoyed at his brother for offering help to the people who left him stranded. "Me and my brother grew up here!" he continued happily.

Stephen parked the truck outside the house and backed up slightly until the car was in line with a garage which was set apart from the rest of the house. Stephen hadn't even turned the engine off before Johnny jumped out of the truck and made his way towards the house.

As soon as Stephen finished manoeuvring the truck, he turned the engine off and climbed out. Dan took his lead and also stepped into the fresh air - followed by Hayley and Charlotte.

"Still no signal," Dan moaned as he shot a quick glance at his mobile phone.

"Really is a nice home you have here," said Hayley - for no other reason than to fill the silence.

"I'll just get the car off and then we'll go back for your friends..."

"Thanks, we really appreciate it," said Charlotte.

"Not a problem," said Stephen. "So you got anyone waiting for you? You need to borrow a phone and let them know you're running late? We have a phone just inside the house," he continued helpfully, "yours if you need it..." Stephen moved to the back of the tow-truck and started lowering the car until all four wheels were back on the floor.

"We're going camping," said Hayley.

"Nice," said Stephen. "Should have just pitched your tents where you ran out of petrol. Could have stayed close to the van and got someone to help with the fuel situation before you were ready to go home again."

"Did cross our minds," said Dan. He slid his mobile phone back into his pocket.

"You should have told me you were bringing back some friends!" called an elderly woman from over by the front door. Stephen rolled his eyes at the sound of his voice.

"My mother, Andrea..." he said. "I apologise now, she doesn't get out much!"

"I'm just helping them out," he called over to his mother. The group turned to see the lady, in her sixties, making her way over to greet them.

"I'm Stephen's mother," she said, "so very nice to meet you all...Are you staying for some dinner?"

"Mum, I'm just helping them out...I don't even know them...They were just parked up on the side of the road...Ran out of petrol. We're going any minute..."

"Going? You've only just got here!" his mother moaned.

"I'm just taking them back to their van and giving them a tow to the nearest petrol station."

Dan stepped forward, "Honestly, if it's a problem - we can make a call and get someone to come and meet us..."

"No!" said Stephen. "It's not a problem. If it was, I'd say so. It's all good."

"Andrea," said Stephen's mother. She extended her hand towards Charlotte. "You are?"

"Charlotte," she took Andrea's hand and shook it. As soon as she let go, Andrea moved to Hayley and did the same.

"Dan," said Dan when Andrea finally got to him.

"It's lovely to meet you all. Now I insist you all stay for dinner," said Andrea. She smiled at Stephen.

"They have friends waiting for them," said Stephen whilst undoing the chain which bound the car to the truck.

"Well I suggest you go and get them," she insisted. "Bring them back here. You can all have something to eat and then be on your way...."

"Thank you," said Dan, "but that won't be necessary. But thank you."

"Nonsense. I insist. Come inside and meet the rest of the family," she took him by the hand and pulled him towards the house. He had no choice but to go with her. "Come along, girls..." Andrea turned back to Stephen who was left standing by the truck, "Run along and fetch their friends," she said, "we'll be waiting."

"Mum, they really don't..." his words fell on deaf ears as the front door slammed shut. He sighed and reattached the chain to the back of his truck to stop it from swinging around when he next drove away.

*

"Please, make yourself at home," Andrea told Dan and the two girls as she led them through to the living room. She pointed them towards the sofa which lined the longest wall of the room. Small coffee tables with lamps were on either side of the settee.

"Thank you," Charlotte said.

"Listen, this really isn't necessary...It was good enough of your son to help us in the first place. We don't want to put you to any further trouble," Dan tried to tell Andrea but she wouldn't hear it.

"It really is no trouble at all," she continued, "it's nice to get visitors. We so rarely get visitors out here. The boys rarely bring anyone home. Their father, Robert, and I actively encourage it too!"

"Is that their dad?" asked Hayley. She was looking at one of the many framed pictures which were nailed to the walls - nearly all of them family related. The picture she pointed to was of Andrea standing next to a tall man who towered over her. The two of them were standing in front of some trees, in a small clearing, with their arms around each other. Both of them looking at the camera with a solemn expression upon their faces as though it were forbidden to smile in any of the photographs.

Andrea was a fairly small lady, with her grey hair and faded blue eyes, but she looked much, much, smaller standing next to the man in the photograph. Hayley considered that it could have just been the angle the photo was taken at but it was most likely the man would be well over six foot tall. Unlike Andrea's all grey hair the man's hair was quite a bit darker, with the exception of his beard which looked as though it belonged on someone else with the amount of grey hairs growing throughout it. Even had it not been for the grey of his beard, the wrinkles on his face would have given away his age - for other than those two factors, you'd be forgiven for thinking he was another son.

"Yes, that's Robert," said Andrea. "That photograph was taken sometime last year," she carried on despite none of the three youths really needing to know. "The picture on the right," she went on, "is of my daughters - Tammy and Suzanne...Tammy is the one on the left; my youngest daughter."

Hayley looked at the picture of the two girls. The same pose as the previous picture and even the same spot. Tammy was standing, taller than her sister despite being the youngest, with her arm around her sister. She had waist length blonde hair. Despite the picture not being a close-up

shot it was clear to see her eyes were of the brightest blue - maybe catching the sun's reflection to make them appear brighter in the photo than they were in real life?

"Pretty," said Hayley, a sting of jealousy flowing through her. Normally she was the prettiest of the girls she hung around with. She wasn't used to someone stealing the limelight from her.

"Very," the mother agreed. "Suzanne's pretty in her own right too," Andrea continued. "Very clever girl."

In the picture, Suzanne was clearly a pretty girl too, let down only by the fact she was standing next to Tammy who'd naturally attract the attention of people looking at the picture. Unlike Tammy, her hair was darker and her eyes, although appearing blue if you looked hard enough, clearly weren't as bright as her sister's.

"How many of you are there?" asked Charlotte.

"There's six in the house," she said. "The two boys, who you've already met, my two girls, Robert and myself. I'm sure they'll be along any minute now. The sound of strangers in the house no doubt luring them from whatever they're up to. Now, can I get you a drink whilst we wait for your friends to arrive? Lemonade?"

"Sure, that would be nice," said Charlotte not wishing to appear rude.

"Three lemonades coming right up," said Andrea. She turned back to the door just as Tammy and Suzanne made an appearance. "Ah, girls, come in...Meet our guests."

"Who you talking to?" asked Tammy - her voice soft and delicate. Another sting of jealousy rushed through every fibre of Hayley as she realised Tammy really was the perfect girl. It didn't help that they were close in age.

"Come in," Andrea repeated herself, "don't loiter in the doorway."

The girls walked into the room and said hello. Hayley couldn't fail to miss the look on Dan's face when he spotted Tammy.

"Hi," he offered his hand for a shake, "pleased to meet you. I'm Danny. Or Dan if you prefer."

"Hi Dan if you prefer," said Tammy. She wasn't stupid. She knew the effect she had on men and already Hayley could see that she was the sort of girl to use it to her advantage.

"Hello," said Charlotte.

"I'll leave you all to get acquainted," said Andrea. "Three lemonades coming right up."

Andrea left the room.

"What brings you out here?" asked Suzanne. "We don't normally get visitors."

"So your mum tells us," said Dan who had suddenly become sociable despite being so quiet earlier when it was just the girls and Andrea. "It's a nice house you have, I'm surprised you don't have more visitors," he did a little laugh as though he had made a great joke. Never once did he remove his eyes from Tammy.

"We broke down," said Hayley - clearly irritated that her boyfriend was attempting to flirt with these girls. "Your brothers found us."

"Oh," said Tammy in such a way it made it painfully obvious to everyone that she didn't really care why they were there. She looked at Dan, "Did you want to look around the house?"

Before Dan could answer her, Andrea came back into the room with a tray of drinks. One for each of the guests and one for her and her daughters. Hayley let out a little sigh of relief. The last thing she wanted to do was go on a guided tour of the house with some bimbo.

"Here we go," said Andrea. She set the tray down on another coffee table; this one was set in front of the settee where everyone was standing. "Please...Take a seat."

Dan and Charlotte sat on the settee. Before Hayley could take her seat, Tammy took it, placing herself next to Dan much to Hayley's annoyance - not that Dan noticed the fact she was clearly irritated. She turned around and sat on one of the other arm chairs whilst Suzanne sat on the last one, leaving her mother to stay standing.

"Hopefully your friends won't be too long," said Andrea. She walked over to the window, which overlooked the front garden, to keep an eye out.

"Are you staying for dinner?" asked Suzanne.

"I believe so - yes," said Dan. Despite his best efforts to get out of the situation earlier, it didn't seem to bother him as much now. Something else that Hayley noticed.

"Yummy," sighed Tammy with a little laugh.

Hayley rolled her eyes.

# CHAPTER SIX

Michael was sitting on the grass verge by the road - the opposite side to where the van had come to an untimely stand-still. He took a puff on his cigarette as he nodded acknowledgement to Joel who was approaching, having left Lara in the van.

"Alright?" he asked.

Joel didn't say anything. He simply took a seat, on the grass, next to Joel.

"Sorry if I've been a prick today," said Joel.

"You're apologising today? What about all the other days you're a prick?" asked Michael, a smile on his face.

"Just feel on edge...It's strange being around Lara again," Joel continued, ignoring Michael's attempt at humour.

"Saw you two talking in the van and thought I'd leave you to it. What's the story with you guys anyway?"

"I'm not sure. I think I still love her?"

"You think?"

"I do."

"You dumped her, man," Michael reminded him.

"Yeah, I know. Regretted it ever since."

"You never said anything. Not to me or the other women you fucked since leaving Lara..."

"Yeah well that'll be our secret. She doesn't need to know about them. They didn't mean anything," Joel whispered. "Besides - what good would it have done talking about it? I only went with the other girls to try and get Lara out of my mind."

"And how'd that work for you?"

"Whilst I fucked the other girls...It's Lara's face I was picturing," said Joel.

Michael looked at him, unsure whether or not he was being serious. "Really? Because...The blonde you shacked up with on the first weekend of being single...She was hot. If I'd known you were going to waste her like that by picturing your ex...I'd have never let you go off with her."

Joel laughed, "You let me?"

"Sure. I was toying with the idea of having her for myself but figured you could do with the pick me up."

"Too generous."

"What are friends for? Man, I can't believe you were thinking about your ex the whole time. What a waste of that girl's good looks."

"Me and Lara - we had a connection," said Joel. His eyes were fixed firmly on Lara, still in the van. She was looking out of the van so Joel only had a view of the back of her head but he didn't care. He hoped she'd turn around and catch him looking. He hoped.

"You had a connection so you dumped her?" asked Michael.

"Well I didn't know about the connection until after I didn't have her."

"So you should have called her."

"And said what? She just said the same thing but what the fuck was I going to say to her? Sorry I dumped you via text but I'm a twat, fancy going back out again?"

"She said the same thing? You told her how you're feeling?" asked Michael.

"That's what we were talking about."

"And how'd she take it?"

"Really well. We made up. Had a kiss. She rubbed my cock and told me she can't wait to be alone with me as there's a lot of angry make-up sex to be had."

"Dude, score!" Michael offered up his hand for a childish 'high-five' moment.

"Mate, I'm taking the piss. How do you think she took it?"

"Not good then?"

"I'm sitting on a damp grass verge with you..."

"Point taken. So what did she say?"

"She needs to think?"

"Ooh," Michael scrunched his face up - not a good sign.

"Ooh?"

"If a woman says she needs time to think or asks for space...It's because she wants...Well..." Michael tried to explain.

"Time to think or some space?"

"Or cock. More precisely...The cocks of other men...."

"Lara isn't like that."

"Push comes to shove all women are like that."

"Even Charlotte?"

Michael didn't say anything. He liked to believe Charlotte was different from the other women and, in his mind, she was; something about her that he couldn't quite put his finger on. In the early days of their friendship, he thought she gave off a different vibe because she was a lesbian. As time went on, he realised this wasn't the case.

"I just think," Joel continued, "she needs space because I let her down so badly. That won't be hard to forget. Or forgive. And I don't expect her to make it easy for me but...Hopefully, in time, we can get back to what we had."

Michael didn't say anything. He took another drag on his cigarette. As he exhaled the smoke, he threw the butt across the road.

"Nothing to say?" asked Joel.

"Me? Like what?"

"We've been friends for years. Just thought...Just thought you might have something to say or some advice or something..."

Michael shook his head, "I just hope it all works out for you," he said. "You talk about anything else?"

Joel shook his head.

"Where the hell are they?" Michael asked. He looked past Joel, down the road in the direction he expected the tow-truck to appear.

"What are you not telling me?" Joel asked Michael. The sheepish look, Michael was desperately trying to hide, was too obvious for even a blind person to miss. "What is it?"

"What? Nothing," said Michael doing his best to avoid eye contact.

"You're lying. What is it? What? Tell me."

"Nothing..."

"There's nothing? We've been friends for years, more than I can remember, God only knows why. I know when you're hiding something. It's written all over your face!"

"I'm just tired...Like you were crabby because you're tired...I guess I look...Look like I'm hiding something when I'm tired?"

"That's bullshit! What is it?" Joel persisted.

"Nothing. Come on, if there was something, I'd tell you."

"We were talking about Lara and you started to...That's it!"

"What?" asked Michael, a flash of panic on his face.

"You don't want me going back out with her," said Joel, with a smug look on his face.

"Yes, yes...That's it."

"Why?"

"Why what?"

"Why don't you want me going back out with her? You think it's a mistake? You think I shouldn't?" Joel continued.

"What? No. No, it's not that at all..."

"It's because he hit on me," said Lara. Joel and Michael both jumped at the sound of her voice; neither of them had heard Lara approach them as they were so engrossed in their conversation - as well as keeping an eye out for the tow-truck.

"He...He what?" asked Joel.

"He hit on me," Lara repeated. "The day you sent me that text message..."

"This true?" Joel turned to Michael with a look of disgust on his face.

"Well...I wouldn't say it happened like that..." Michael knew, out of everything he had ever annoyed Joel with, this would be the thing that killed their friendship - something he wanted to avoid.

"You hit on her?"

"He did," Lara confirmed.

"What did you say to her?" asked Joel.

"I just thought," Michael thought on his feet to find the perfect excuse, "I just thought she might have been suicidal...She loved you, man. She loved you."

"Suicidal?" asked Lara - almost offended. "You think I'd kill myself over him? I'm that weak? Fuck you..."

"I thought you might have wanted to go out and have a laugh...Take your mind off things," Michael butted in, trying his best at doing all round damage control. "I was trying to be a friend!"

Lara reached into her pocket and pulled out her mobile phone. "Trying to be a friend?" she asked. She started to flick through her messages.

Michael remembered the message he sent her. Another flash of panic across his face. "Well, obviously...If you were feeling low...I mean you could have read more into it."

"Makes sense," said Joel.

"And fuck you too," said Lara - still frantically flicking through her messages. "Here...Here it is." She handed the phone to Michael, "Does that ring any bells to you?"

Michael didn't say anything.

"Show me," said Joel.

"Okay, so...I think I remember sending it now...Yes...I was drunk. Definitely drunk. Extremely...And very...Disgustingly drunk. In fact, how I didn't end up in hospital that night...With permanent liver damage is..."

"Show me the text message, Michael." He didn't wait for Michael to do as instructed, he simply reached across and snatched the phone from his hands. "Drunk?"

"Definitely."

"You sent the message at two in the afternoon," Joel showed him the message again.

"Alcoholic! That's me."

"You're a piece of shit, really. How have we been friends for so long? How have I not seen this before? Truly. A piece of shit."

"Ah, come on, man...You dumped her. Fair game."

"You tried to fuck my girlfriend and that's all you can say?"

"She wasn't your girlfriend when I tried to fuck her, to be fair. And when you were together...I never once thought about it. Because friends don't do that to each other."

"You know what? I don't want to hear this. You and me...We're done," said Joel. He passed the phone back to

Lara and got up from where he was sitting on the grass verge. He walked over to the van and climbed in.

"Was that entirely necessary?" Michael asked Lara. "He didn't need to know. It's not as though anything happened between us. What was the point of doing that?"

"Because it's what you deserve," said Lara. She tucked the phone back into her jeans pocket and followed Joel to the camper van.

"That's fucking great," said Michael. "Thanks for that. Brilliant. Now I'm talking to myself..."

A horn sounded off from down the road. Michael turned his head to see the oncoming tow-truck returning from dropping the car off.

*

Stephen was driving the tow-truck. Michael was sitting next to him, with his head leaning against the window, staring at the world passing by.

Lara and Joel were sitting in the back - an all too obvious distance between them.

A few more silent minutes passed by slowly before Michael leaned forward and flicked on the radio.

# CHAPTER SEVEN

"What are we doing here?" asked Joel when they finally pulled onto the family property where Dan, Hayley and Charlotte were already waiting.

"Oh, finally, it speaks!" said Stephen sarcastically. He pulled the tow-truck up in front of the old house.

"Come on, I'm not in the mood for games...What are we doing here?" Joel continued.

"Collecting the others," Michael muttered. "You think he dropped the car off here and then dropped the others off at the petrol station to wait for us?"

Stephen twisted in his seat to address everyone in the truck, "You're really the life and soul of the party, aren't you? Yes, your friends are here...But, we're not going to the petrol station right away..."

"Why doesn't that surprise me. Why not?" said Joel, fed up with the constant delays in getting to the campsite - although part of him just wanted to go home now.

"Because you're staying for dinner," said Stephen in a matter of fact tone. "My mother insisted, your friends agreed."

"Brilliant!" moaned Joel ungratefully.

Stephen turned to him with a stern look on his face; for the first time since introducing himself to the group, he even sounded annoyed, "I suggest you don't use that tone when you give thanks to my mother...And give thanks you will."

Joel's face flushed, "I'm sorry," he said, "it's just been one of those days."

"That's not my fault," Stephen pointed out, "nor is it my mother's fault so...Play nice...Unless you want me to take you back to where I found you and just leave you there?" he raised an eyebrow.

"No. I'm sorry. I didn't mean to cause any offence."

Stephen suddenly smiled, "Come...Let me introduce you to the family."

With no more words, Stephen opened the door and jumped down from the tow-truck.

Michael laughed, "You certainly told him!"

"Just fuck off, Mike...Seriously fuck off!" Joel hissed. He opened the door and stepped out - slamming it behind him, despite Lara needing to get out too.

"This is your fault," Michael pointed out to Lara. "You at least going to cheer him up by agreeing to go out with him again?"

"Don't you get it yet, Michael? None of us like you. Why do you insist on hanging out with us? We can barely tolerate you."

"Yeah, okay, if you say so...I'm sure you're all big enough and ugly enough...Certainly ugly enough...To tell me to leave if you didn't want me around."

Lara leaned forward, into the front of the truck, and whispered slowly and clearly, "We don't want you around anymore. Take the hint." She didn't wait for his response, she just left the truck via the same door Joel had used.

"You coming?" called Stephen from the front door.

Michael nodded and followed.

*

Dan was still sitting next to Tammy, on the sofa, along with Charlotte. Suzanne and Hayley were still in the armchairs with Andrea standing next to the window.

"Looks like your friends are here," Andrea pointed out.

Tammy jumped up from her place on the sofa and joined Andrea at the window to see the new visitors - a sneaky glimpse before she had to meet them face to face. Hayley took the opportunity of the empty place on the sofa next to her man to swap seats.

"Jump in my grave just as quick?" Tammy asked with a cheeky grin on her face.

Hayley flashed her perfect white teeth at her in the most fake smile she had ever used. She managed to not blurt out, "No, I'd just piss on it," although she desperately wanted to.

Suzanne couldn't resist getting a sneaky look at the other guests either and joined the others at the window, just as Michael disappeared into the house. "They all staying for dinner?" she asked.

"Of course," said Andrea - a welcoming smile on her face.

Dan tried to get out of it, once more, although he knew it was pointless, "Really, it isn't a problem."

"I know it isn't," Andrea quickly replied. "Honestly, we'd love to have you for dinner."

"I'll start preparing the vegetables," said Suzanne as she left the room.

"Can we at least help?" asked Charlotte.

"No, no..." said Andrea. "It won't take her anytime at all."

Charlotte smiled at her despite feeling awkward at how generous the family were being.

Stephen stepped into the modestly decorated room, "Hello again," he said to the house guests, "look who I found loitering out on the road," he turned around and waved Joel, Michael and Lara in.

"And what are your names?" asked Andrea.

Joel did the introductions, "I'm Joel, this is Lara and this is Michael."

"Pleased to meet you," said Michael - remembering what Stephen had said about playing nice to his mother.

"I'm Andrea, this is Tammy...You've just missed my other daughter, Suzanne. She's just popped into the kitchen to prepare the vegetables."

"Thank you for this, this is lovely," said Lara taking heed of Stephen's words too.

"It's lovely for us too," said Andrea. "Anyway, if you'd like to take a seat - we'll go and start getting things ready. Stephen, you can help..."

"I've just got in, mum, haven't I done enough for today? It is supposed to be my day off after all! Do I not do enough during the week?"

"More hands make idle work. And spuds don't peal themselves," said Andrea as she pushed him towards the living room door - followed by Tammy who gave a sly wink, which didn't go unnoticed, at Dan.

"What the fuck was that about?" asked Hayley as the living room door closed.

"You've either got it, or you haven't..." teased Dan, "...And I clearly have it."

"What the fuck is any of this about?" asked Joel. "Someone want to explain how we ended up having dinner with these guys?"

"They were very persistent," said Charlotte.

"I thought we were going camping. Clearly I was mistaken!" Joel sat on one of the spare armchairs.

"What harm does it do?" said Michael. "We're already late..."

"No thanks to you," Joel butted in.

Michael ignored him, "I'm just saying we may as well make the best of a bad situation. If these people offered

dinner...We should accept. Not only is it free but it saves having to stop off later on."

"Later on? That's if we even get there today. We need to get the van sorted and they're out there cutting up potatoes. Clearly their idea of dinner isn't a round of sandwiches."

"Which makes it all the better. I, for one, am hungry...Besides, I tried to tell her not to worry about it," Dan chipped in.

"I think we should just go," said Hayley.

"Let's just eat their food. Say thank you. Get a lift. We don't have to stay for hours and hours!" said Charlotte. "It'll be fine. It could even be quite nice."

"I agree with Hayley, this just feels wrong!" Joel argued.

"You lot listen to yourselves? Yes they're strangers but, at the end of the day, they're just being kind and helping us out. What's wrong with that?" said Charlotte.

"Let's just see what they make, eat it...Stay long enough to be polite, and then get to the petrol station," said Michael. "We can still get to the site in a few hours. We can make this part of the holiday. Besides...That girl looks nice...Right Dan?"

Dan grinned from ear to ear fully aware that she did look nice and that she had also been flirting with him.

Joel didn't share his enthusiasm, "Is there anyone you wouldn't fuck, Michael? Jesus Christ..."

"Me!" Lara pointed out. "But only because I said no, right?"

"I told you..." Michael went to defend himself but was cut off mid-sentence.

"Fine, we'll stay for dinner...We'll get a lift to the petrol station but after that we're going home!" hissed Joel.

"What?" asked Dan. "Home? What about the weekend we had planned?"

"I think we should cut our losses...I mean, is anyone even still in the mood for it? I, for one, am not. I don't want to spend any more time with him," Joel pointed to Michael.

"For fuck sakes! I'm sorry!" said Michael - not keen on losing a friend nor his weekend away, especially as he had walked out of a job to make sure he could attend it.

"What for?" asked Joel. "Are you sorry for getting us in this position, in the first place, or are you sorry for trying to fuck Lara?"

"What? Whoa there...Have we missed something?" asked Dan.

"Wouldn't be surprised," said Hayley, "you've had your eyes fixed firmly on that slut's breasts since she introduced herself and tried giving you a lap dance?"

"What? Oh, come on, don't you start...I was being friendly...They were being friendly to us! What was I supposed to do?" asked Dan.

"I think we all need to just calm down a little," said Charlotte, "let's not forget where we are..."

They all fell silent.

"Look, I just want to eat the meal and go home. If you lot want to go on to the site, you can...I'm just not in the mood for any further little adventures this weekend," said Joel eventually.

"Fine, if that's what you want," said Dan. "I think it's a shame but I won't twist your arm." He addressed the rest of the group, "What about the rest of you? What do you want to do?"

"I think things have been said and done already which would make for an unpleasant weekend," said Lara. "I agree with Joel."

"You can answer that but you can't answer whether you want to go out with him again though?" spat Michael

seizing his opportunity to make her feel as uncomfortable as him.

Dan, Charlotte and Hayley all turned to Lara, surprised to learn Joel had asked her out again.

"Fuck you," hissed Lara.

"Didn't we establish that was never going to happen?" said Joel, backing up Lara - although part of him had hoped it would prompt her to give him an answer.

"Fine! We'll all go home!" said Michael. "But I think you're being retarded! This was all nothing more than a mere speed bump. The text was taken out of context and the fact I got us lost...Just a mistake...You want to punish everyone because of that...Fine. Be my guest. But that's your choice so fuck you."

The living room door opened and Andrea walked in with a tray of drinks, "See - it never takes long when there's more than one of you in the kitchen. And they say too many chefs ruin the broth. Proof in the pudding that this isn't the case." She put the tray down on the table opposite the group, "Are you having fun? Sorry to be so anti-social...We just want to ensure dinner is ready in a timely fashion...No doubt you're all keen to get going!"

"It's fine," said Joel, trying his best to keep a civil tone in his voice despite his blackened mood. "We have all the time in the world," he finished.

"That's lovely, dear," Andrea replied. "Well enjoy your drinks, you must be parched, and I'll be back to check on you in a bit." She finished what she was saying but she didn't leave. She simply stood there, in front of them, watching the glasses. Eventually the youths took the hint and took up a glass each.

"Thank you," they all muttered before taking a sip each to keep her happy.

"My pleasure," she said. She smiled and walked from the room, closing the living room door behind her.

# CHAPTER EIGHT

Dan opened his eyes and sat bolt upright when he realised he was lying on a bed. Tammy was sitting on the end of it looking at him with a genuine look of concern on her face.

"Are you okay?" she asked.

"Where am I? What happened?" he asked. He looked around the decidedly pink bedroom; pink duvet, pink pillow cases, pink walls. Definitely her room. "Where the hell am I?"

"It's okay," said Tammy. "You're in my bedroom." She saw the look of panic on her face and went onto explain, "My dad put you in here after you fainted downstairs."

"I fainted?"

"Banged your head pretty hard on the side too. We were worried."

"I fainted?" he repeated. He rubbed his head as though it'd help with the banging headache he had pounding the inside of his skull. "Where's Hayley?" he asked.

"She's downstairs. They all are. They're eating. I excused myself to go to the toilet. Wanted to make sure you were okay. They told me to leave you be but...I wanted to check. Is that bad?"

"What? No...No, it's fine. Thank you. Fainted you say?"

She nodded, "You mentioned something about feeling funny one minute and the next, you dropped like a sack of spuds. How are you feeling now?"

He shook his head, "Okay I guess...I don't remember anything. I best go and make my apologies."

Tammy slid up the bed, closer to him, and pushed him back down so his head was on the pillow, "There's no rush, is there?" she asked. "I've been wanting to get you to myself since I first saw you. Thought you looked tasty..."

"Tasty?" he laughed. "People still say that?"

"I do," she nodded. She laid down next to him. "Kiss me?"

"What?"

"Please. I want to taste you. Kiss me." She didn't wait for him to answer. She kissed him on the mouth. A small peck to start off with. He kissed her back and she opened her mouth, slightly, to grant access to his wandering tongue.

"You taste good," she said at the first opportunity. She moved back in for another kiss but Dan stopped her.

"Wait."

"What is it?" she asked. She looked more confused than hurt. As though she didn't normally get men stopping her from kissing them.

"I have a girlfriend. She's downstairs...You're beautiful...Really you are but I can't do this..." he said.

"I won't tell if you don't," she purred. She kissed him on the right cheek whilst stroking her hand down his left. The hand didn't stop there, and neither did her mouth. She kissed his mouth again, encouraging him to kiss her back, whilst her hand moved down his body. Down his strong chest, across his stomach and over his crotch. "Do you want me to stop? It doesn't feel as though you want me to," she whispered.

Dan sighed with pleasure and kissed her again whilst she fumbled with his belt. Seconds later she freed his erect penis.

"It'll be our secret," she whispered as she started to stroke his hard shaft. "Do you want me to kiss it?"

Dan was squirming on the bed with pleasure. He nodded without hesitation. Tammy smiled and kissed him

again before positioning herself so she was sat on top of his chest, her hand reaching behind her - refusing to release her grip on his cock. She laughed as she repositioned her body so that she was sitting on his legs - making it hard for him to move, not that he had any intention of moving away from her. Seconds later her warm mouth enveloped his manhood. He sighed with pleasure again as her saliva trickled over his helmet with a gentle flick of her tongue.

"That feels so good," he moaned.

Tammy looked up and sucked her way to the tip of his cock before letting it slip out of her mouth, "I want to taste you," she said.

"Don't stop, please..." he sighed.

Tammy smiled and continued to suck on his member, much to Dan's delight.

"Ouch," he suddenly sat upright. "Less teeth," he whispered, still nervous of anyone catching them.

Despite having his penis in her mouth, Tammy couldn't help but smile at his request.

"Tammy," he whispered as he tried to get her attention as he felt she couldn't have heard him. "Tammy," he repeated. He looked down to where her head was bobbing up and down. When he whispered her name for a third time,

she opened her eyes and looked him directly in the eye. "You're hurting me," he whispered, a frantic look in his eye and a quiver in his voice despite his best efforts to hide it from Tammy for fear of offending her.

Tammy didn't release his penis from her mouth, instead she closed her eyes and - within a split second - clamped her teeth down, with enough force to ensure the top row met up with the bottom, before twisting her head to the side as hard as she possibly could, tearing his member from his body with an awful ripping sound that was nearly drowned out by his loud, ear-piercing scream. Blood spraying everywhere. She sat upright, her jaws chewing, with a devilish look in her perfect blue eyes. Had Dan been able to open his eyes he'd have been able to see a complete look of euphoria upon her pretty, but bloodied, face. A few determined chews before she took a hard swallow. Dan continued screaming, with his complexion getting paler, as Tammy sucked her fingers clean.

"You taste amazing," she said, "nom nom nom." She moved down his writhing body, back to where his appendage used to be, and stuck her tongue into the still bleeding hole. Dan's shrieks of pain and terror abruptly stopped as shock, and blood loss, forced him into a state of

unconsciousness - not that Tammy cared as she continued to lick at the blood as though she were a cat lapping up a bowl of delicious fresh milk.

A few more minutes of frenzied drinking and she moved back up to be face to face with him, "Why'd you have to fall unconscious? You missed the best bit." She sighed, "They always do." She prised his mouth open and tentatively reached in, with two fingers, and took hold of his tongue. With it firmly between her fingers, she pulled it out of his mouth and touched it with her own tongue, "Kiss me," she purred. She made the tongue flap up and down, using her fingers, and matched its actions with her own tongue. "I knew you'd be a good kisser," she said when she eventually stopped. She couldn't help but laugh as she took his tongue between her teeth. She released her fingers and started to slowly move her head backwards until Dan's tongue was stretched as far as it could possibly stretch.

The same mischievous grin spread across her face as it had done earlier. She took a hold of his tongue, once more, and informed him, "These are two of my favourite things," she said. "The first..." she used her head to point downwards to his crotch, "...You can't beat it. But, the

second best bit?" she smiled again and gave Dan's tongue a short, sharp tug - ripping it from his mouth. "Perfect!"

She tilted her head back, opened her mouth, and dropped the piece of tongue onto her own. She held it there for a moment to savor the flavour, "Oh my, how did you have this in your mouth for all these years and not get tempted to swallow it yourself? I don't think I could have done it. Although, I'm not entirely sure how feasible it would have been to actually eat it yourself..." She looked at Dan. There was absolutely no colour in his complexion at all, other than the traces of slowly drying blood she had inadvertently wiped on his skin whilst getting close to him, and his chest was barely moving up and down. "You're not listening to me at all, are you?" she said, a slight hint of disappointment in her voice that her playmate was already near death. She carried on chewing, occasionally sucking, on the tongue before swallowing it down her throat. "Yummy!"

A knock on the door shattered her euphoric bliss and made her jump.

"Who is it?" she asked.

"It's me," said Johnny. "Can I come in?"

"Hang on!"

Tammy jumped off the bed and pulled the duvet from underneath Dan, with some effort. As soon as he was clear of it she threw it over his dying body to hide what she had been doing. A quick look around the room to make sure everything was okay. She nodded with satisfaction. If she just stood in the doorway, to greet her brother, he wouldn't be able to see the blood which had sprayed the wall next to her bed.

Another knock on the door.

Tammy casually walked over to the door and opened it ever so slightly - enough for her brother to see her but not enough for him to see into the room without having to strain past her and, even if he did, the blood wouldn't be as noticeable as a body on her bed.

"You've been snacking, haven't you?" he said.

"What? No. What are you talking about?"

He pointed to her face which, she had forgotten, was coated in bits of Dan. Johnny pushed past her and stepped into the bedroom, "What have you been doing?" he asked when he stopped by the blood splatter on the wall. His eyes fixed on the lump underneath the duvet - the duvet which was also starting to show blood slowly seeping through it. "What the hell, Tammy?"

"Don't tell dad!"

"Not sure how we're going to hide this," he said. He pulled back the duvet and saw the full horror of what she had been doing whilst left to her own devices. "Fuck...Was he at least still drugged whilst you...Well...That...." he pointed to where Dan's penis used to be. Tammy looked to the floor in shame. "Brutal."

"I got carried away."

"Yeah, you did. Damn Tammy, you know mum hates it when we snack between meals. And this...This is just wasteful. You know she's preparing dinner as we speak right now, right? We won't get through that and this before it goes bad. I don't even want to know what dad is going to say."

"We could hide the body," Tammy said, suddenly, as she desperately clutched at straws.

"You know that won't work."

"Could make it look as though he ran away?"

"They wouldn't stop looking for him. They'd be too afraid he'd bring someone back to help his friends. Jesus Christ, what were you thinking?"

"I was hungry!"

"And you couldn't wait a couple more hours? Or even have a biscuit? We can't hide this from mum and dad."

Tammy sat on the bed, deflated. The bliss she had from the taste of flesh was all but a distant memory now as she realised the disappointment and anger she'd cause her parents when they discovered what she had done.

"You're better off telling them sooner rather than later," said Johnny, "you never know, she may not have started preparing the meat...Could save her selection for another day." He paused, "Do you want me to tell them?"

Tammy nodded. A scared little girl.

\*

Even though the picture of Robert made him out to be tall - it'd still have come as a shock had you seen him face to face for the picture didn't do his true height, six foot five inches, any kind of justice. He was an imposing figure with muscles clearly bulging under his tight v-neck t'shirts, despite the fact he was in his sixties. His face, mostly hidden behind a shaggy grey beard which didn't match the colour of the hair on his head, permanently seemed to have

a scowl upon it - something which made his height even more scary in reality.

He was standing in an old wooden barn, set back behind the house, muttering to himself whilst skinning a deer which hung from the barn's rickety rafters. Hayley was hanging, next to the deer, by her feet. A look of sheer panic on her gagged face. Robert pulled the knife he was using, from the deer's carcass, and gave the blade a careful lick.

"Dad?"

Johnny's voice from the barn's doorway startled Robert, not that it showed.

"Didn't I tell you not to disturb me whilst I'm working, boy?"

Johnny didn't answer him. Instead he waited, with Tammy by his side, for his father to turn to face him - something which didn't take long. Robert noticed the state of Tammy's face immediately.

"Speak!" he demanded.

"I'm sorry, dad," she whispered.

"What's happened?" he asked. "Who's blood is that?"

Tammy didn't say anything for he knew what his temper was like and could tell he was already in one of those moods she had known from when she was a youngster

- and had always feared so much. Johnny stepped in to help his sister.

"It's the guy we put in her bedroom," Johnny said.

"What about him?" Robert demanded.

"He tried to run," Johnny lied. Tammy didn't deny it. Instead she let her brother continue lying for her. "She didn't have a choice..." he insisted.

"Where is he now?" Robert asked.

"He's in the bedroom..." said Johnny. "She didn't have a choice..."

Robert snarled as he pushed his way past his children to see what had happened. He knew the only way of knowing for sure was to see with his own eyes.

# CHAPTER NINE

Tammy was sitting at a large kitchen table with tears in her eyes. Her face was still bloodied from her earlier feeding frenzy. Her hands rested, shaking, on the table surrounded by various bowls of vegetables.

Johnny was sitting with her, "It'll be fine," he told her.

The door opened revealing Robert and Andrea. Both of them looked angry.

"I'm sorry," Tammy said to them.

Robert didn't say anything. He crossed the room towards her in two single steps. He raised his hand, high in the air, and brought it down hard on Tammy's face causing her to scream in pain.

"Don't fucking touch her!" hissed Johnny. He leapt off his seat with his fists clenched, as though ready to strike back.

"Stop it!" screamed Andrea from the doorway where she had remained. "It's not the end of the world. I haven't started on the meat yet...Nothing's been wasted. I'm sure I can salvage something."

"What's wrong with you?" asked Robert.

"He tried to run," said Tammy - fighting back her tears.

"Rubbish!" shouted her father. "We saw what you did. He hadn't tried to run and he wouldn't have either...Not all the time you had a mouthful." He looked as though he wanted to hit her again. "Or did you do that?" he asked Johnny who was still standing next to him - ready to take his swing.

"Fuck you!" hissed Johnny.

"And where were you last night? Cruising for more cock? You're an embarrassment."

"I'm not gay! How many times do I have to keep telling you?"

"Prove it!" Robert spat back. "Prove to me that you're a man."

"What?"

Robert grabbed Tammy by the hair and lifted her to her feet. Both Johnny and Andrea screamed for him to stop but he didn't. He pushed her down on the table and pulled her jeans down using a swift, forceful, movement with his spare hand. "I said prove to me how much of a man you really are," he hissed - a look of pure hatred and evil burning from his eyes.

Tammy screamed, "Get off! Please! I'm sorry!"

"Ssh," Robert lifted her head off the table and slammed it back down - stunning her into silence. He turned his attention back to Johnny, "Well, boy, what are you waiting for. Stick her. Come on! Look at that tight, pretty little cunt...Doesn't that make you hard? Don't just stare at it...Fuck it!" he demanded. Keeping her head pinned to the table with one hand, he pulled her knickers to one side using the other - revealing her vagina to Johnny.

Johnny screamed at his father. Not from fear but more so out of hatred for his dad. He turned and fled the room hoping that Andrea would talk Robert down from his rage.

"Robert, please..." said Andrea, "you're scaring us...Please..."

"No balls," hissed Robert. "And he says he ain't a faggot?"

"Robert, please..." Andrea continued.

"Shut up, whore. Something inside of you... Something... You did something to make him like that. Something broke him whilst he was cooking in you. Should have fucking stamped on the little shit as soon as you spat him out. Should have. Still should. Do us all a favour. One less mouth to feed." Using his spare hand, he pulled at his

Johnny stormed into the dining room and slammed the door behind him. Without taking the time to look around the room he punched the wall as hard as he could - in his mind the plaster was his father. In his mind the crack in the plaster was a crack in his father's face. The blood, from his knuckles, also belonged to his dad - in his fragile mind. He hit the wall again. And again. Each punch working out more of his frustration and anger at not being able to stand up to his own father. He knew someone had to. He knew someone had to put him in his place. For the sake of the family. He just wished he were strong enough. He went to swing at the wall again and suddenly froze when something, in the room, caught his eye. Slowly he turned to face the dining room table; a large oak table in the middle of the room with enough chairs, around it, to seat the entire family.

On the table, with two tall candles on either side of her, was Charlotte – naked, bound by restraints holding her wrists and ankles - a ball gag in her mouth and make-up smudged down her pretty face from the tears of fear which leaked from her eyes uncontrollably.

He stormed over to her and spat in her face. "This is your fault," he whispered so as not to alert the rest of his family that he was talking to the dinner, "if we hadn't picked you and your friends up...If we hadn't..." he stopped talking and just stared at her naked body, suddenly overcome by lust. "I'm not gay!" he hissed at her as though she had been the one to name call him in the first place. "I'm not."

Charlotte squirmed against the restraints as she felt her captor clamber up onto the table next to her. She couldn't help but wonder what he was doing. She kept her eyes closed tightly. If she couldn't see him, perhaps he wasn't really there? She knew it wasn't the case. She knew but hoped nevertheless.

He whispered in her ear, "I'm not gay. He wants me to prove it?" His gravely voice sent a shiver down to the base of her bare spine. "You smell good," he continued, "Fresh...A hint of fear. Fear is good." He nuzzled her neck and breathed in deeply - taking his time to take in her natural scent. "Mmmm..." he laughed, "....Good enough to eat. Good enough to fuck."

He kissed his way down her chest. He stopped long enough to give her nipples a little flick with his tongue. She let out a sigh; one of surprise and not pleasure.

The restraints were straining as she pulled and twisted against them harder – straining, but not giving.

Her captor kissed down her stomach, another flick of his tongue - this time across her belly button. Hardly a pause before he continued moving southwards. A kiss against her pubic area. A small moan escaped his lips. A small whimper of panic, as she realised what was to come, from hers. He moved lower until his head was between her legs. A pause. She could feel his rancid breath against her vagina.

The restraints still refused to budge from her desperate squirming.

He breathed in deeply and sighed once more.

She clenched, bracing herself for what was to come; another flick of his tongue. Perhaps an experimental probing of his index finger? Nothing came. She opened her eyes and looked down. He was still there, between her legs. He was looking up at her. His eyes almost black in this light. Soulless. The lust and hunger overshadowing

previous thoughts of despair and hatred for his father. He smiled.

"You smell great," he repeated. He continued looking at her as he moved himself lower. He stopped just before he reached her knee and promptly ran his tongue up the inside of her quivering thigh.

The damned restraints not allowing any freedom. She couldn't help but whimper. Tears of fear turned to those of disgust as they ran down her pale cheeks.

He stopped when he reached her vagina again.

A lick of his lips.

"Salty. Your fear tastes salty. One can only imagine what that'll do to the flavour of..."

He ran his hand up the inside of leg, where he had just licked. Whereas his face had stopped just before her vagina, his hand didn't. His determined fingers ran across her labia.

"Please don't..." she mumbled around the ball-gag but he ignored her. His fingers forcing themselves to slowly part her lips. His breath so close that she knew it was only a matter of seconds before she'd feel his lips against her skin again.

He suddenly stopped and withdrew his fingers.

She opened her eyes in time to see him climb from the table with a look of shame on his face. His eyes back to a more normal colour as though he had come to his senses - brought back, with a bump, by his own guilty conscience.

"No," he whispered - more or less to himself. "No." He turned and hurried from the room, closing the door behind him.

Charlotte couldn't help but let slip with a sigh of relief even though she knew it was far from over. She called out, "Somebody help me!" despite knowing the chances of anyone coming to her aid were slim.

\*

Tammy was in her bedroom, against Dan's corpse, crying on the soiled bed. Suzanne was sitting on the side of the bed trying to comfort her.

"What's happened?" she asked. "What is it? Tell me..." Suzanne didn't need Tammy to say what was causing the tears. She knew only too well. She had been in the same position herself. She recognised the limp that Tammy walked with when she passed Suzanne's bedroom to get to her own room. It was a limp she had walked with on many

occasions - usually late at night after her father had paid her a visit, drunk on the taste of flesh. For him to attack Tammy without even a hint of the taste of flesh, without even taking a taste of what was to come...Clearly he was already in a frenzied mood. Suzanne put her arm around Tammy but still Tammy didn't say what was wrong. She just buried her face against Suzanne's chest as though it was a safe haven from any monsters looming.

There was a gentle knock on the door.

"Come in," Suzanne called out - she hoped that, whoever it was, they'd be able to have more success in calming Tammy down.

Johnny pushed the door open, "Can I come in?"

Suzanne nodded. Johnny stepped into the room and shut the door behind him, after a quick look to make sure his father wasn't nearby.

"Are you okay?" he asked Tammy. He had partly felt responsible for what had happened. It had been his idea to tell their parents what Tammy had done - not that they had had much of a choice. She didn't respond. "We need to do something about him..." It didn't matter that Suzanne heard him. He knew she had suffered at the hands of Robert too.

They all had. "We shouldn't have to live like this...In fear of him..."

"It's not him," said Suzanne.

"Bullshit, who else is it?"

"You know who."

"No, I don't believe in that. And you don't either," he retorted.

"Maybe we should," she continued.

"Believe in what?" asked Tammy, wiping away the tears from her cheeks.

"You don't remember the stories dad told us as we were growing up?" asked Suzanne.

She shook her head.

"Don't even start, Suzanne...None of it...It's not true. It's just stories. Some little tribes in North America... Around that area... Stories to tell their children...To scare them away from what we have grown up enjoying..."

"Tell me," Tammy insisted.

"I don't think our dad is always himself," said Suzanne. "He used to tell us of a legend...Told by...I think...Algonquian people...The legend of Wendigo..."

"Why are you telling her this? You don't believe in it...You said so yourself."

"Maybe I was wrong. We were wrong." She continued, "A malevolent spirit that could possess humans. People who were...People who liked...What we like...Flesh...Human flesh...We are more at risk."

"Then why haven't we been possessed?"

"I don't know. Perhaps because he has been doing it for longer. They say that, when possessed, you'd become violent and obsessed with eating human flesh...You know how hungry he can get...You know how violent he can get too."

Tammy started to cry again, "But...I couldn't stop myself either."

"What do you mean?"

"I knew I shouldn't have done what I did but I couldn't stop myself. From the moment they got here...I knew what I wanted and, at the first opportunity, I took it."

"It's not the same," said Suzanne. "You were just hungry. We all are. It's been months since we've had a good meal. A proper meal. Other meat just doesn't satisfy the cravings as much. You are not like him, though. None of us are. We wouldn't hurt each other...We wouldn't. How many times has he hurt you?"

"I forgot."

"I try to too," nodded Suzanne. "Too many times to count. Too many times to forget. He isn't our father anymore. He is something else."

"So you agree we need to do something then?" Johnny butted in.

Suzanne nodded, "What about Stephen and mum though?"

"They're either with us or against us."

"And what about our guests?" Suzanne enquired further.

Johnny smiled, "I'm sure we'll work up a hunger."

\*

"Who's that?" asked Joel with a hint of fear in his voice. He was tied to a chair with ropes around his wrists and ankles. Unbeknownst to him, in the same position behind him was Lara.

"Joel? Is that you?"

"Lara?" Joel tried to turn his head to see her but couldn't. "What's going on?" he asked.

"I don't know," she replied - the same fear in her voice. "I just woke up here. What happened?"

"I'm the same. Just woke up. Can you see anything?" he asked.

"No."

They were sitting in one of the house's many rooms - not that they knew that as all the lights were off and there appeared to be no windows to let in any light or glimpse of their surroundings.

"I'm scared," Lara whispered.

Joel wanted to tell her that everything was okay. He wanted to tell her that he'd protect her from whoever did this to them. He wanted to say it but didn't because he knew it would've been nothing more than a lie - a lie which would have been easy for anyone to detect.

"Me too," he whispered back.

"Where are the others?"

Again, he didn't answer. Lara didn't expect him to. It was more of a rhetorical question. After all, in the position he was in, there was no way for him to know where any of their friends were. He startled to struggle against the ropes which had him locked to the wooden chair.

"What are you doing?" she asked.

"Can you get your hands free?" he replied as he still battled against his restraints.

"I don't know," she started to fight against her ropes too. "They're tight," she moaned.

"Fuck!"

"What is it?" she asked.

"Nothing. I cut myself on the rope. Fuck!" he said again. "What the fuck is going on? Where are we?"

"I don't know!" said Lara. She started to cry as fear took hold of her senses.

"Lara, it's okay. It's okay. Just try and remember. Do you remember anything before waking up here?" he asked. "Anything at all?"

"I just remember that we were waiting for dinner. The old lady...She gave us some drinks and we drank."

"The lemonade," Joel suddenly realised what had happened, "it was drugged."

"What? It couldn't have been. She wouldn't have!"

"She wouldn't? You don't even know her."

"And you do? She seemed nice. They all did."

"That doesn't mean anything," he pointed out to her. "Obviously there's some fucked up family shit going on in here and we're slap bang in the middle of it." He started to fight against the ropes again, despite the damage they were doing to his wrists.

"What are you doing?" asked Lara. The more Joel fought against the ropes, the more he was bumping into her back.

"We can't just sit here and wait for whoever it is to come back. We need to get out of here. And now."

"What about the others?"

"They're probably trying to get out too," he pointed out. "If they're even alive."

"What?!" another flood of panic rushed through her body.

"Nothing. I'm being dramatic. Come on, we need to get out of here. Can you get your hands free? Anything? If one of us can get out...We can help the other..." he continued. "Before they come back!"

Light flooded into the room as the door suddenly opened - giving both Lara and Joel a view of their prison; a derelict room. No carpets, just wooden floorboards. No wallpaper, or even paint, just bricks. There was nothing. When Lara's eyes adjusted to the sudden light, in the room, she noticed Stephen standing in the doorway.

"Hi," he said. "Can I get you guys anything to eat or drink?"

"Quick!" whispered Joel, when he realised it was Stephen standing in the doorway. "Undo the ropes."

Stephen laughed, "Undo them? It took me ages to do them up - why the Hell would I want to undo them?"

"Please..." said Lara.

"Oh ssh now!" said Stephen. "I came here, in good spirits, asking you if you fancied anything to eat. I didn't come for an argument. Now, are you hungry or not?" He stepped into the room.

"Of course we don't, you sick fuck. We want to go home...What are you playing at? What do you want?" shouted Joel.

"Okay, for your own sake, I'd stop shouting...You don't want to disturb my da...." Stephen was cut off mid-sentence as the door slammed behind him plunging them all into darkness. "What the hell was that?" The door's lock clicked shut. "Great!" He twisted the door handle but the door, unsurprisingly didn't budge, "Okay, very funny... Come on...Let me out..." He pressed his ear to the door and listened as, whoever had closed it, walked further away from them. He banged on the door but the fading footsteps on the other side didn't falter. "Brilliant!" he muttered.

"Let me out," said Joel as he seized the opportunity, "we can force the door together...We can all get out."

"Seriously...I'm in a good mood...It's probably just my brother mucking about...Don't ruin my good mood. Shut up!" Stephen warned.

Joel fell quiet.

\*

On the other side of the door, Johnny quietly crept away - back down the hallway he had previously snuck up, to catch his brother unaware. He turned the corner and bumped into his sisters.

"Well?" asked Suzanne.

Johnny held the key up that he had used to trap his brother.

"You didn't talk to him?" asked Tammy.

"Even if he agreed with our plan - we don't need him. It's easier this way...We'll deal with him afterwards..."

"He might be angry," said Suzanne.

"And we'll deal with him afterwards!" Johnny snapped. "What would you do if he didn't agree with us? Back down? Carry on living as we are now?" The girls

didn't answer. "This is easier. It's better," he pointed out. "trust me. This is for the best of the family. How long before his temper...His greed...How long before he decides he's permitted to snack on his kids?" They knew he was right. "Look...Let's just get this done, yeah? You want it too, right?"

There was a slight pause before they both nodded.

He pushed past them and walked down the stairs. The two girls followed close behind - both of them starting to feel nervous about what was to come.

# CHAPTER TEN

The knife slid into Hayley's face as though it were as soft as butter. She didn't scream though. The knife's first cut, across her throat, made sure she made no noise now - other than a strange gurgling noise coming from her mouth - and, more importantly, the first cut ensured she didn't move around whilst Robert continued working on her body.

The knife moved down slowly so as not to prematurely tear the flesh off the bone. The blade was pulled upwards when it got to her chin - an action which ensured the piece of skin was cut cleanly off.

"Perfect!" sighed Robert as he held the flap of skin up to his eyes for a closer look. "Should have been a butcher!" He opened his mouth and stuck his tongue out - dropping Hayley's skin onto the middle of it. Another sigh escaped his mouth.

"Robert?"

He stopped chewing, "Robert?" he said. "Is that any way to speak to your father?" he didn't turn around to see who was addressing him from the doorway to the barn. He

didn't need to. He recognised the insolence in the tone as Johnny's.

"I'm ashamed you're my father," Johnny said. Had Robert turned around he'd have seen that Johnny was holding an extremely large knife.

"The question is, though..." said Robert whilst preparing another piece of Hayley's flesh for mastication, "...are you as ashamed of me as I am of you? My own son...Disloyal...Disobedient...Disappointing..."

"Coming from a rapist? You fuck your own daughter," Johnny hissed.

"Daughters!" Suzanne pointed out.

Robert stood upright. He had no idea Suzanne was standing next to Johnny. Slowly he turned around as he popped the next piece of skin into his mouth. He saw Tammy was there too.

Johnny looked at Suzanne, "I had no idea," he said.

"It's not something you brag about."

"You're standing with him?" Robert asked. He spotted the knife, "And what do you plan to do with that? Oh I see. You've come to put an end to my evil ways..."

"You're not our father. You haven't been for a long time," said Johnny.

"Oh? So who am I?" asked Robert - trying his best to hide his smirk.

"Wendigo!" Tammy pointed out.

"Wendigo?" Robert laughed.

Tammy nodded.

"You're not well," Suzanne whispered.

"You want to know where I went yesterday? I left. I had a bag packed and I jumped into my car. I left here. I left you all. The only reason I came back is because the car broke down..."

Robert stared at her with a look of contempt on his face. How dare his own children talk to him as though he were mentally ill. After the briefest of silences he asked, "You think I'm ill?"

"You have been for a long time," said Johnny as he took a step forward with the knife clutched firmly in his hand.

"You think I need to be put out of my misery?" Robert went on to ask.

"It ends. Now." Johnny said.

"Yes," his father agreed, "I do believe it does." He smiled. "Well, come on then boy, make your move."

Johnny paused. He looked at his sisters for encouragement - a sign that it was still the right thing to do. They both were watching their father intently. He guessed that, if either of them were opposed to the idea, they'd have already said something.

"There is just one thing though," said Robert, "if I really am Wendigo, as you all seem to suspect, how do you think a knife is going to kill me? I mean, we're supposed to have hearts of ice... Us Wendigo monsters...The only way to kill us is with a hot bullet through the heart. Do you remember anything I taught you?"

Johnny hesitated for a moment or two. Long enough for Robert to lunge forward and plunge his own knife straight into Johnny's heart. Suzanne and Tammy screamed whilst Johnny just stood there with a startled look upon his face. He opened his mouth, as though he wanted to say something, but no words came - just blood trickling down his chin.

"You're no son of mine," hissed Robert as the life faded from Johnny's clouding eyes. He let go of the knife - his own bodyweight stopping Johnny from dropping to the floor - and Johnny dropped to his knees. Knees first and then face forward; the force of the handle hitting the floor

so hard it made the tip of the knife stick out of Johnny's back. Robert spat on Johnny's body and turned to his daughters who just stood there - too scared to do, or try, anything. "I believe it's dinner time," he whispered; a tone so threatening they didn't dare to make a move of their own. He pushed past the girls and out of the barn.

"What now?" asked Tammy.

*

"Please...I won't tell anyone...Please...Just let me go...Please...I beg you..." Charlotte was squirming against the restraints which kept her bound to the table where Johnny had previously left her. She was positioned, in such a way, on the table that her head was in front of Robert who was sitting at the head of the table, casually tucking a napkin into the top of his shirt - no doubt in preparation for unavoidable crumbs being spilt.

Andrea was sitting at the other end of the table - the raw deal as she had the end with Charlotte's feet. Tammy and Suzanne were sitting on the sides, opposite one another. There was an empty seat where Johnny and Stephen should have been. The girls, and Andrea, were weeping for Johnny.

"Am I to presume Stephen didn't want any part of your plan?" Robert asked as he continued adjusting his napkin. "I take it his body is somewhere around the house?" The girls didn't answer. "A shame. He was a good son. At least I was able to count on one child out of four." He looked to Andrea, "Did you know of their plan?" he asked - all the time trying to ignore the pleas of Charlotte.

"I swear, I didn't..."

"Perhaps you even put them up to it?" he interrupted her.

Charlotte screamed.

"I suppose I have been strict," he continued ignoring Charlotte's scream as though he were used to it, "but I have been so for your own good. I had to protect the family. What I did...What I do...It's always been for the good of the family as a collective. But I don't suppose you give a shit, do you?"

"Please..." Charlotte whispered looking directly at Robert.

He finally snapped, "I'm trying to have a conversation with my family," he hissed. "You trying to talk over the top of me...It's rude...Very fucking rude...Now...I'd be eternally grateful if you'd shut up. Food should be eaten and not

heard!" He addressed the rest of the family, "Right now we should be eating as kings and queens. All of us. A family. A real family. Enough food to last us for months but you've all played your part in ruining that for each of us."

"I won't tell anyone...I won't....I promise..." Charlotte pressed her luck. "Whatever I've done...I'm sorry."

"It's nice to get fresh food eaten like this," Robert sighed, "but it's a real pain in the arse when it doesn't know its place and continues to yak. Shut...Up...." he bellowed.

"Maybe we should just eat," said Andrea. "It might make us feel better."

"For once we agree upon something," said Robert. He leaned forward until his face was nearly touching Charlotte's, "Now you can start screaming," he told her.

He sat upright and put his hand over one of Charlotte's eyes. As soon as his skin touched her's she let out a little scream of fright. A louder scream followed when he dug his fingers into her eye-socket. By the time he removed them, he had her left eye in the palm of his hand. Charlotte's screams got louder and louder - the pain from her eye so unbearable she probably didn't notice the girls were pulling back her finger nails in a tried and tested method for removing them completely so they wouldn't get stuck in

their throats. Robert slid the eyeball into his mouth and held it there for a second before pressing down with his teeth to the satisfying sound of a pop. A little juice squirted down his chin much to his amusement. He had barely swallowed when he pressed his hand back against Charlotte's face.

\*

"What's happening down there?" Joel asked from the darkness of the room where he was trapped with Lara and Stephen.

"It's dinner time," Stephen answered as though it were all perfectly normal.

"What's that supposed to mean? Dinner time..."

"That sounds like Charlotte," said Lara - her voice quivering with fright. "What are they doing to her? What's happening?"

"I'm more concerned with how come they're eating and yet I'm still locked in here," said Stephen. He stumbled his way, through the blackness, to the locked door and started to bang on it as Charlotte screamed on downstairs. "Hello? Anyone? Come on! I'm hungry too! Why aren't you letting me out? A joke's a joke...Come on!"

"My friend is in trouble," Joel pointed out, "let me out so I can help her! Please!"

"Now why would I want to do a thing like that?" asked Stephen. He carried on banging the door, "I'm supposed to be down there with them!" he reminded Joel and Lara.

"They're eating her?" asked Lara as another loud scream echoed through the house.

"I'd say so - yes," said Stephen. "They'd better save me some that's all I can say."

"You're fucking nuts! The lot of you!" Lara cried.

"We're nuts?"

"You eat people?"

"We're nuts?" Stephen repeated. "You're nuts! You haven't even tried it! If you had - you'd realise you were the crazy ones for going so long without trying it! It's the best fucking meat in the world. Tastes so good. One taste - you never forget. Tell you what, if they've left any..." another scream filled the room, "...I'll sneak some up for you to try. Fair's fair..."

"You're sick!" Joel shouted.

"I was sick," Stephen pointed out, "when I was young. I was about five or six, if memory serves correctly, and I

caught some disease. Doctors didn't know what it was. They had me wired to all these machines in the hospital...My chances of survival, they said, were slim to none. My dad...My dad unplugged me from that bed and took me home. He didn't want me dying in some strange hospital bed. Once home he stayed with me, day in and day out...He fed me this meat...A strange taste which I had never known before but loved...A week later, on this strange diet, and I had enough strength to leave the bed. Two weeks later I was running around in the woods with my younger brother...Years later, occasionally getting another taste of that strange meat, my dad took me into the barn where he had been preparing it...He told me what it was. He showed me. A person. I didn't know who it was. Some stranger. He had taken them. Skinned them. Fed them to his family. At first I was disgusted. I wanted to run but I didn't. I was so young - where would I have gone? Mother was there, to reassure me it was okay. She told me they were bad people and it was their way of making amends for their wicked ways - they'd give themselves up to offer us strength in our hours of need. And strength they did give us...None of us...None...We never got ill. Not even a cold. We gained the strength and protection of those whom we devoured...Our

own medication to keep us safe in this disease-ridden world..." He started to laugh, "I'm sorry, I can't keep it up. I'm just playing with you...We just like the taste. Seriously...I mean it...If they leave any of your friend...I'll get you some to try. Can't say fairer than that." He started to laugh when, suddenly, he saw a shadow in the darkness lunge at him. Before he had time to react a fist, hard as concrete, connected to his face causing him to stumble back blindly.

"What's happening?" Lara screamed when she heard the commotion - unaware that Joel had managed to free himself from his ropes.

Stephen stood up, propping himself against the wall, in time for another fist to connect - this time to his stomach. A punch, so hard, it took the wind from him but he didn't have time to react or attempt to catch his breath as a knee connected to his face; a loud crack from the bridge of his nose as the bone splintered under the skin. No relent. No forgiveness. Another knee directly in the same place as the last. Another. And another. By the time the blows stopping coming, Stephen slumped to the floor barely conscious. The last thing he saw, through instantly blackened eyes, was a large size eleven foot heading down towards his face.

"Joel?" Lara asked when the banging and crashing came to a stop. There was silence. "Joel?"

"Yeah," he said - out of breath. "Talk to me..." he said.

"Is he dead?" she asked. Joel used the sound of his voice to find his way back to where Lara was tied to the chair. "Joel?" she asked again, "Did you kill him?"

"I think so. I hope so," he told her as he fumbled with the ropes which bound her. He stopped when another of Charlotte's screams ripped through the house. "We have to get out of here," he said. He carried on with the ropes.

"What about the others?"

"What about them?" he asked. "They're probably already dead...And if they're not dead yet," he said as another scream pointed out that at least one of them was still alive, "they'll be dead soon."

"We can't just leave them," said Lara.

"When I said I wanted us to be together...I didn't mean in a stew!" he said.

"I'm not leaving them," she said as the ropes were pulled away from her wrists. He leant forward and started to undo the ones around her ankles. "If you love me - you'll help me..."

"This is fucking insane," he said. "You know that, right? This whole situation...We need to get out of here. We need to...We can get help for them when we're out!" he told her.

"I can't leave it...Them...They're our friends."

"Fine!" he said. "But the first sign of trouble or even a hint that they're dead...We leave."

"Yes," she said. She dropped the ropes to the floor - free at last.

# CHAPTER ELEVEN

Charlotte was lying motionless on the table - chunks of flesh missing from her body in various places, two deep black holes where her pretty eyes used to be. The majority of the flesh was missing from Robert's end of the body.

"What's the matter," he asked as he swallowed the last piece he had in his mouth, "you're not hungry? Be a shame to waste her."

Suzanne looked at Robert whilst nibbling on one of Charlotte's fingers - which she had already bitten off. "You just killed our brother...Her son..."

"You were there, Suzanne, it was kill or be killed. Right? Right?" He wiped the excess blood from around his mouth using a part of his napkin. "What do you think?" he asked Andrea.

"I just wish we could have talked..."

"That's what we're doing now."

"Talked before anything happened," she went on. "We used to talk."

"They killed Stephen...Your other son...The three of them...They plotted together...Fucking killed..."

"He's not dead," Suzanne snapped, breaking Robert's flow.

"Oh? Then where the fuck is he? He wouldn't miss out on a meal!"

"He's upstairs. Johnny locked him in with the two...." Tammy explained.

"He's alive? Go and get him then. Before dinner gets cold," said Robert. "And then the five of us...We can all sit here and sort this mess out once and for all. Like a proper family!"

Andrea stood up, "I'm going to start preparing pudding," she informed the family. She wiped another tear from her face and walked from the room - not that anyone acknowledged her. They were all too busy staring at each other; Suzanne and Tammy watching their father and he was eye-balling them right back.

"Well? Go and get him," he ordered the girls. They both stood up, to see his orders through, "Not you," he pointed to Tammy, "you can wait here...Keep your old man company so I don't get lonely."

"I'll be right back," Suzanne told Tammy. She gave her a sympathetic smile. She knew that leaving Tammy with their father was a bad idea but also knew there was no

choice without further angering him. Tammy smiled back and Suzanne left the room.

"You know," said Robert, "the whole Wendigo thing is bullshit, right?" Tammy looked at him. "It's a myth. A legend. A story to scare people into not eating Human Flesh. Why they'd want to deny their loved ones something that tastes so good is beyond me, though, it really is...You think...You think if your brother had managed to kill me - do you think you'd have still eaten flesh in years to come?" Tammy didn't answer. "Yes. I think you would. You like the taste too much, don't you? I've seen you feasting...The look in your eye. Sheer joy. Pleasure. The taste dancing around...Teasing your taste buds...Exploding your senses...Delightful, isn't it?"

"Fuck you," Tammy hissed.

"Whoa," said Robert, "check out my little firecracker. I think that's the first time you've ever sworn at me...But, come on, we'll all chat...Tomorrow...You'll realise how silly you've all been. But, don't worry, I won't hold a grudge. I'm not that sort of person. I'm more of a..."

"Rapist!" Tammy snapped.

Robert stood up and walked over to where Tammy was sat. He leaned down close to her and whispered, "It's

funny how that's only a problem now the rest of the family know. You've never complained before. If memory serves correctly...Sometimes..."

"Shut up!"

"In fact, the first time we ever fucked..."

"Shut up!" she continued - louder this time.

"You begged me. When I found you in the car...With your date...He was in the back seat...I need to remind you of how he was? Trousers around his ankle...A slash across his throat...Blood in his lap...You on the back seat next to him...Little panties pulled to one side, rubbing yourself with what appeared to be a piece of his member... Moaning... Sighing... The blood around your mouth...The look in your eyes..."

"SHUT UP!" Tammy screamed.

"You begged me to fuck you. Remember that? Begged."

"No..."

"And now the family know we've fucked..."

"You raped me in front of my brother and my mother..."

"You always liked it rough," Robert reminded her. "Those nights you told me to come to your room...You'd

whisper it in my ear before you'd go upstairs to bed...Whisper it so the rest of the family wouldn't hear. You know, after feasting on flesh...Your sister...Suzanne...She's the same. Begs me. Must be an alpha-male thing."

"What?"

"You didn't know? You didn't compare notes?"

"You never fucked her in front of the rest of the family!" Tammy shouted again. "How am I supposed to look them in the eye now?"

"That's what the problem is? All the times we've fucked...All those times...Now...Now you feel bad about it? Now you think it's wrong? And now you think I deserve to die?"

"Johnny was right. You're not our father anymore."

"No. I thought we were something more," he said. "You and I have always had a special connection but...Well...Now it appears I'm condemned to death. Is that because you want to fuck your brothers now? Younger? Better looking Is that the real reason you were so happy to go along with Johnny's stupid little plan?" He paused. "God only knows what was going on in your sister's head. Probably jealous that I sleep with you. Rather see me dead than know we're lovers too."

The door suddenly swung open with so much force it hit the wall with a bang. Robert and Tammy span around to see what caused it; Suzanne was standing there with a knife pressed against her throat. Hiding behind her were Joel and Lara.

Lara screamed when she saw Charlotte's body.

"Dad!" shouted Suzanne.

Robert stood up, "What the fuck is this?"

"Where are our friends?" demanded Joel.

"Well - there's a little of one of them on the table...If you give us a few days...You can probably fish the rest of them out of the toilet bowl..."

"Dad - please?" continued Suzanne.

"Oh - now I'm your father?"

"I'm not joking," shouted Joel, "where are they? Tell me or she's dead."

"Kill her. I was only going to kill her later. You'll be doing me a favour."

"What? Dad?"

Robert noticed the knife for the first time, "The knife...You've been in the kitchen? What have you done with my wife?"

"What?"

"The woman...In the fucking kitchen..."

"There was no one there," said Lara - unable to take her eyes off her friend's half-eaten body. "Please...We just want to go home."

"You're not going home, okay?" said Robert. "You know it. I know it."

"Where are our fucking friends?!" shouted Joel. He pressed the knife against Suzanne's throat harder causing a little bit of blood to trickle down her neck. She let out a squeal of pain.

"Daddy - please..."

"Just kill her already," said Robert - a smile on his face. "If you can't kill her...How are you going to kill me? Think of her as the practice run before you come to me...I'm Wendigo, don't you know?" he laughed and winked at Tammy. A laugh cut short by Joel's scream.

Robert turned his attention back to Joel just in time to see him drag the knife across his daughter's throat. Suzanne's eyes went wide as panic set in - a jet spray of blood spurted from the slit all across the dining room floor. Tammy screamed whilst Robert applauded, "Well done, you, I didn't think you had it in you..." Joel pushed Suzanne to one side, where upon she fell to the floor clutching

hopelessly at her throat, and made a sudden dash forward for Tammy who did little to protect herself from the incoming attack. The knife's blade pierced her skin as easily as it had slid across her sister's - a funny sound from Tammy's mouth, as opposed to a scream, to let all those around realise it was a serious impaling. Robert howled with laughter as he jumped to his feet. "What a day this is turning out to be!" he laughed.

Joel pulled the knife from Tammy's chest, where he had stuck it for a second time, and looked at Robert who was still standing by his seat.

"You really should have given your friend a weapon too," Robert said - a menacing tone in his voice and his eyes fixed on Joel. "You think you can get to me before I can get to her? Look at her skinny little neck...No weapon to protect herself from me...It won't take much for me to snap her neck. I may be older than you but I bet I can move quicker," he winked at Joel. "Really should have given her a wea..."

Joel cut him short, "Get out, Lara. Go and get help."

"I'm not leaving you."

"Oh how noble," Robert teased.

"Just go!" he insisted.

"But you better run fast, little girl, because I'm right behind you," Robert smiled and did a biting motion with his mouth. "Working up quite an appetite here."

"Fuck you!" hissed Lara.

"A lot of people saying that to me today," Robert pointed out. "They're all dead now. Just saying. The two might not be related but, if they are, you're fucked."

"Fuck you!" she reiterated.

Robert laughed.

Lara turned and ran from the room - straight back into the hallway and towards the front door. She didn't look back as she hurried towards it. Once there, she twisted the handle only to find it was locked. The sound of a car engine outside, followed by a wheel-spin. Someone clearly in a hurry to leave the property.

She tried the handle again on the off chance it was just stiff, "Fuck!" The kitchen, she thought, could have had a back door. Without knowing how much time she had to spare, she hurried back down the hallway into the kitchen where the stench of gas hit her. A quick glance at the hobs - everything was on, even the oven which had been left open. No time to worry about that as a crash came from the dining

room. She rushed over to the back door and pulled at it but it didn't budge - locked just as the front door had been.

Joel screamed from the other room.

"Come on, please!" she screamed at the door as she continued to tug at the handle in the hope it would magically unlock itself.

"We rarely keep that door unlocked," said Robert from behind her.

She span around and screamed when she saw him standing in the doorway, coated in blood and clutching the knife.

"Don't be so afraid," he said, "it's not my blood… You'll be pleased to hear… I'm actually okay… Although, I don't think your friend is going to make it if I'm going to be honest." He did his best to give a sympathetic smile before he started to laugh. He took a step closer, "Just so you know...I'm really going to enjoy eating you." Lara started to cry. "Oh, don't cry...Makes the skin all salty...I've been trying my best to keep salt out of my diet. My wife...She says it's bad for you and, well, apparently it is. See, I didn't know if she was telling the truth so I looked it up. Apparently too much salt is definitely bad for you."

"Why are you doing this?"

He took another step closer.

"Because I can!" Robert said. He held the knife up and waved it at her. "Now, you going to save me the effort and come to me or are you going to make me come all the way over there?"

Lara, panicked, looked over to the wall where she saw a light switch. With a final scream she lunged forward and hit it with her elbow - her eyes closed tightly as though it would protect her from the explosion...She opened her eyes. The lights were on. There was no explosion.

Robert smiled and walked over to the hobs where he turned everything off, "The gas needs enough time to build up pressure," he informed her. "All this has succeeded in is making you look stupid and giving me a headache... So... Yeah... Well done for that." He opened the window above the kitchen sink. "Be fine when we let a little air in."

Lara screamed as Robert suddenly rushed towards her - the knife held outright.

# CHAPTER TWELVE

Andrea felt her face redden. Standing in the queue, to pay for the petrol for her son's truck, she realised she'd left her purse at home by leaving in such a hurry.

"Next!" said the cashier having waved the last customer off.

"I'm sorry," said Andrea, "I've just realised..." She whispered so as not to be overheard by the customers behind her which would only embarrass her further, "I've left my purse at home."

"Failed to see the sign then?" asked the cashier with an expression on his face which implied he had heard it all before.

"Which one would that be?"

"The one that warns you to make sure you have enough money to pay before using the pumps?" the cashier continued. A smug look on his face as though he was enjoying Andrea's embarrassed squirming. "We just need you to fill in a form," he said.

"A form?" she watched as the lanky cashier jumped up from his stool to fetch a form from across the other side of where he was serving. "What kind of form?"

"Name, address, phone number...That sort of thing. Gives us your details so we know you'll be coming back to make the payment at some point."

"Oh, I see. My home address?"

"That would be the one," he passed the form over to Andrea, along with a half-chewed blue ballpoint pen, "there you go."

Andrea hesitated for a second.

"We have your car registration on camera so the police would know where to find you - this is just a back-up," the cashier informed her - aware that she didn't seem in a hurry to pass over her details.

"The police?"

The cashier nodded, "Sometimes we get people who don't pay for their petrol. Clearly you're not one of those people. Obviously you've just left your purse at home, like you said, but...Sometimes..."

Andrea started to fill in her details. The cashier turned away to serve those waiting in the queue behind her. Andrea knew she couldn't go home to get her purse. For years she

had wanted to run away from the terrors under the roof but she was always too afraid to make a run for it just in case they found her trying to run - her husband, more to the point. Instead she just went along with the way he ruled the house to keep the peace. It was safer that way. She didn't want to end up as a meal and it wasn't as though they didn't eat well. It certainly was a delicious taste, when they managed to bring the meat home.

At the start it all began so innocently. A hunting accident during a deepfreeze. The worst the country had seen for well over a decade with the deepest snow they'd ever seen themselves. They couldn't get out to go and get food. The snow and ice lasted for months and the problem with living in the middle of nowhere was that the routes to their house were rarely salted making it hard to venture out for supplies. The body of their middle son was just sitting there, in the barn - even after their cupboards ran dry. To start off with - it was a necessity - but, afterwards, it became a simple pleasure. With the taste so good it was easy to forget what it was - or who it was.

Over the years they tried cooking the meat in various ways but they always found the best way to eat it was raw - whilst the person was still living and breathing. Andrea

knew it was wrong but she couldn't stop herself. The taste of the meat was too good to pass up and it squashed any thoughts of right and wrong. Until recently that is. Recently she was starting to think of themselves as the monsters they really were. She didn't believe in stories of Wendigo, or other such creatures, but she knew that people like her husband and her belonged in Hell. Now, today, she wished she could take it all back. She wished they had all starved when the food did run out, during that deepfreeze. Often she even found herself wondering whether they would have gone hungry or whether they could have made it until the thaw - a thought she always tried to suppress for she knew it was pointless to think like that.

She couldn't remember how she was talked into eating the people alive. She couldn't even remember if it was her who needed convincing. Part of her thought it could have been her who convinced the others to do it. The greed of human flesh robbing her of any sane thoughts? There was even talk of opening their own restaurant where other people could come and dine on the delights of humans - something they often joked about as they sat around, on a Sunday afternoon, making up potential menus.

"Adam's Apple Crumble," she muttered to herself with a smile on her face.

"I'm sorry?" the cashier asked as he walked back over to her.

She snapped back to reality, "Nothing. I'm sorry. Here."

She had put a fake address down on the sheet which she handed back to the cashier. She had no intention of going home to get the money just in case her husband was still alive and she was dragged back into the argument. She had made it this far and was damned if she was going back just to try and get away from them again. She decided she'd have to raise the money some other way. Find the money to pay the cashier back before the police were alerted. She didn't want to go home but she knew she couldn't have the police go there either.

If her husband had survived, or any of the other family members had survived, she knew it would be bad enough with them hunting for her. She didn't need the police hunting her too. That would have been too much.

"Thank you," said the cashier. He placed the form on the side.

A fake address to slow them down if she didn't manage to get back, with some cash, in the next twenty-four hours. She'd make it back. She had to. She gave the cashier a fake smile and left the petrol station.

She jumped into the front seat of the car, turned the ignition, and drove from the forecourt. She drove for a few miles down the road, with various scenarios running through her head, before she suddenly pulled the car over to one side. Nervously she climbed out and walked around to the boot. She opened it up and looked inside, "I'm sorry," she said, "I'm going to need to borrow some money."

Michael laid in the boot, his hands and feet bound and a gag around his mouth...His eyes full of fear.

- END

Enjoyed the stories? Check out Vimeo for some of Matt Shaw's short films!

https://vimeo.com/themattshaw

Want more Matt Shaw?

Sign up for his Patreon Page!

www.patreon.com/themattshaw

Signed goodies?

Head for his store!

www.mattshawpublications.co.uk

Made in United States
Orlando, FL
12 March 2025

59395535R00097